CAELUM

A House of Ausher Novella

EMBER DRAKE

HE'S THE INCUBUS OF
YOUR DREAMS.

CAELUM

A HOUSE OF AUSHER NOVELLA

EMBER DRAKE

First paperback edition 2024

*Book cover design by Ember Drake on Book Brush and
Canva.*

ISBN 979-8-9902478-2-6 (paperback)

CHAPTER 1

I t was such a simple, tender thing, their first kiss.

Caelum had been wanting to court her for some time now. He thought she was some divine being sent from the heavens, and he knew he wanted to her be his. He had asked his caregiver and guardian for permission to court her properly. His guardian, his savior, was hesitant at first. Caelum was a young incubus who had yet to mature and come into his powers. However, Zaven, who was going by the name or Roland Ausher while he was in the mortal realm, could not deny the pleading look of a young man enthralled by what was to be his first love.

The girl's name was Aideen Brenan. She had eyes like glittering emeralds, skin like fresh crème, and hair like a capture blazed. She was a spirited Irish girl with a smile that could light up a room. The weeks he spent wooing the girl were magical, to say the least. Despite his rough start to life—and its subsequent end—he found a purpose. Caelum wanted nothing more than to see Aideen smiling always. Each time he saw her, his heart swelled.

Soon, the day of his sixteenth birthday came. Roland had reminded him to be careful now that he had reached the age of maturity for incubi. His powers could activate at any time. Caelum agreed to be mindful of them, but he had other things on his mind. Aideen had told him she had something special for him for his birthday.

They had spent nearly every day in each other's company, meeting secretly at the Three Cliffs Bay. It was where they always met because it was a beautiful central location to where they both lived in Swansea, Wales. They tucked themselves away in the ruins of Pennard Castle, not too far from the beach. It was their special place where they talked and laughed while the will-o-wisps flitted about.

There was nothing particularly special about the day, his sixteenth birthday. It was a rather dreary day, but that did not put a damper on his mood. He was going to see his love, his Aideen. When he arrived at the ruins, she greeted him in the broken archway that was the entrance. She was a vision in a simple, pale green dress, with her wild, untamed head of rust-colored curls that shone under the light of the afternoon sun. What little of it there was. Aideen welcomed him into her arms and planted a chaste kiss on his flushed cheek. She led him into the ruins, her small, delicate hand in his. When they arrived at her intended destination, she released his hand and turned to him with the biggest smile on her freckled face. There, on the ground, was a large red blanket with a bottle of wine and a bowl of fresh strawberries and grapes. He wondered where the clever little thief had nicked them from. It would have been just like her to have snatched the goods from an unsuspecting home. He smiled knowingly.

Caelum was still unsure of himself around others. His power had yet to present itself, and it worried him if it ever would. Would people ever suspect him of being a monster? There was still a standing order to have his kind killed on the spot. He told Aideen what he was, but the girl had no fear of anything. Especially him. He wanted nothing more than to spend the rest of his life with her, but she was only human and did not live for long. His demonic blood was too strong within him. He would live for several centuries.

"Wat's wit the sour face?" she asked, snapping him out of his thoughts.

"Hm? Oh, it's nothing," he blushed.

She had removed the distance between them, and now was only a hair's breadth away from him, her bright smile shining up at him.

It was so cute, the way she crinkled her nose when she suspected him of lying. Her smile was gone now. Her luscious lips were now in a full pout. His mouth suddenly felt dry, and her lips were a welcomed oasis.

"Caelum Evans! Wat on earth is goin' t'rough yer head?"

His eyes shot open, and his mouth gaped. "Nothing! I swear!"

"Liar!" she grinned. "Ya were t'inkin' 'bout me gettin' all old and wrinkly again. Weren't ya?"

"No," he laughed. "I was thinking nothing of the sort."

She eyed him suspiciously. "Then wat were ya t'inkin' 'bout?"

"I was thinking that I would love you no matter how old and wrinkly you'd get."

She tapped him on the arm and laughed. "C'mon, before the critters get to the food," she smiled, turning back to the picnic.

Though she was rough around the edges, and nothing like a proper lady, he adored her. He wanted her to be his for however long she had. "Let's run off together," he offered, grabbing her by the hand before she could sit.

"Are ya daft?" she laughed, turning back to him. "Where would we go?"

"We could go to London. Didn't you say you've always wanted to see the tower?"

"Yes, but–"

He gently pulled her into his embrace. "I don't care where we go, so long as we're together."

4

She giggled at that.

"I'm serious, Aideen. I want to marry you and have a life together."

Her smile faded a bit. "Oi know ya do. Oi want that too, but..."

"But what? If you're worried about money, I'll find work."

"No! Wat if someone found out 'bout ya?"

He smiled at her. It was the first time he had seen her worried. "No one will find out. We'll be fine."

"I don't know..." she murmured, avoiding his eyes.

"Please, trust me. I will take care of you always," he pleaded softly.

She lifted her gaze to his, her eyes twinkling with the threat of tears. "Do ya really fancy me enough to marry?"

He grinned ruefully. "You are the most perfect woman in the world. Of course, I fancy you enough to marry you."

The tears broke free and ran down her flushed cheeks. "Ya promise?"

"With all my heart," he smiled warmly.

"Then yes, Oi'll marry ya," she squeaked out.

With a sharp inhale, he captured her lips with his. It was their first kiss, and it was perfect. He pulled her tighter against him, and, had it not been for their clothes, he would not have known where he ended and she began. Caelum found that every part of him wanted to be in contact with her. As if he meant to absorb her into himself. The moment he released her, his mouth hovered over hers. An ethereal strand of light came floating out of her mouth and into his. He could see the white glow of his eyes reflected in hers, but the sudden hunger consumed him as he consumed her. She smelled of fresh honey, and tasted even sweeter. Her vitality made him buzz all over with unfamiliar power. It was exhilarating! And he only wanted more, and she was not fighting him. By the time he could stop himself, it was already too late. The slip of a girl was now a husk in his arms. Her once supple, pale skin was now dry and gray, wrapped tightly around small bones. Her lips were thin and cracked, and her face had sunken in. The rusty red hair that adorned her head was now dull and lifeless, the curls gone.

When he snapped out of the haze of his lust, a frigid chill ran down his spine. He shook, falling to his knees with Aideen still in his arms, as a sob caught in his throat. Burying his face in her brittle hair and clutching her tight to his chest, he broke down. He rocked back and forth as he cried, apologizing as he did so.

Caelum was unsure for how long he had sat there with her body cradled in his arms, but it had been for a while. The sun was setting. He did not know what he would do. There was no way he could take her to her parents. He could not explain what had happened without outing himself as an incubus. Though he did not want to live without Aideen, he did not want to be executed either. Then it hit him.

He wrapped Aideen in the blanket she had brought for their picnic and carefully carried her back to his home. It was dark when he arrived at the manor, but not so late that Lynnox was asleep. The small woman greeted him at the door and regarded him with concern as she closed the door behind him.

"Caelum? Dear, what happened?" she asked as tears welled up in his blue-green eyes.

"Roland!" he cried. "I need Roland!"

He held Aideen's body tighter when Lynnox tried to take her from him.

"All right, I'll fetch him for ya," she replied softly, then hurried off out of the entryway.

After a few minutes, Lynnox returned to the entrance with Roland. Caelum was kneeling on the floor with Aideen's body crushed against him as he sobbed into her hair. He felt Lynnox's small, gentle hand on his shoulder. He had looked up and saw Roland standing before him. Roland was average height with a slender but muscular build. He had dark hair that ran just past his ears and always looked wet. It was his eyes that startled Caelum. They were normally a cold, dead brown, but when he looked down at Caelum, they were soft and sad.

"What happened, boy?" he asked softly, kneeling in front of him.

Caelum stared blankly for a moment. He was not sure how to explain what had happened, just that Aideen was gone. And all he did was kiss her.

"But you can bring her back, right? Like you did for me."

Roland sighed and shook his head. "I'm sorry, lad, but I can't. She's been gone too long. Her soul has left her body."

"How can you be sure?" he shouted. "You haven't seen her!"

There was a low rumble of a growl, and Roland's eyes flared in anger for a moment, but softened at the sight of Caelum's distraught face.

"I am Death, boy," he stated flatly. "I know when a soul has left its body."

"No! She can't be gone!" Caelum cried out.

"I'm sorry, Cae, but she is," Roland replied.

Caelum felt his body go numb. The world seemed to stop as he stared ahead, unseeing, as Roland's words echoed in his mind. His heart raced, and he felt a crushing weight on his chest. The memories of his time with Aideen flooded his mind—her laugh, her smile, her brazen way of living... their first kiss. Fresh tears welled up in his eyes. He barely felt when Roland removed Aideen from his arms. He just let it happen. There was no point in holding on to her any longer. She was gone. It was his fault. He killed her. His love.

"Caelum, breathe!" shouted Lynnox, shaking him furiously.

But he could barely hear her calling him. She sounded so distant. Then everything went black.

When Caelum woke up, the sun was setting again. For a moment, he thought he had died. Part of him wished he had. He had taken a life. The life of his only love.

"Oh, good! Yer awake," came Lynnox's soft, motherly voice.

Caelum sat up and stared blankly at her.

Lynnox wrung her hands together with a worried expression.

"What happened?" he asked.

"Ya were grievin', love, ya fainted," she explained. "Ya should stay in bed a while longer. Ya need the rest."

"What happened to Aideen?"

"Oh," she said, as she briefly avoided his eyes. "Zaven took care of her. He took her back to her folks and told them he found her alone like that."

It was his turn to avoid her gaze.

"It's all right, love. It was an accident. Ya didn't mean to... hurt her," she tried.

"You mean kill her? I killed her, Nox." He turned his attention to his window. "Sure, it was an accident, but I still did it. I need to turn myself in."

"You'll do no such thing," said Roland, coming into the room. "I didn't save your life just so you could end it again."

"If you hadn't saved me all those years ago, Aideen would still be alive," he countered.

"Ya don't know that," spoke Lynnox.

"You're sad and angry. I understand that better than you know, but ending your life wouldn't bring her

9

back or make you feel any better," Roland explained, his tone even but stern. "All you can do now is atone for the life you've taken. Learn control of your power, live, and remember her. But for now, stay out of sight until the search for what happened to her is over. Hopefully, you two were careful about not being seen together."

Caelum balled his hands into fists around his blanket as he stared daggers at Roland. He knew Roland was right, but he was hurting. His ears were hot and ringing so loud with anger that he had not heard when Roland spoke.

"Answer me, boy," he said calmly. "Will you stay hidden and live for the girl?"

"Yes," he growled, sniffling. "I will remain hidden and live for her."

"Good," he sighed. "Come down for supper if you're up for it."

Caelum turned back to his window, hearing Lynnox sigh as she and Roland left. He was not hungry, and he could not bear the company or others at that moment. He wanted to be alone, but he realized that as long as he stayed in Roland's house, he would not have any privacy. It would soon be dark enough when he could venture out without being seen.

It did not surprise Caelum when he stepped out of his room that there was a tray of food waiting at the door for him. Although Lynnox always made sure Caelum was well cared for, Caelum still found he had no appetite... at least not for food. It was all he could do to stifle his growing lustful urges. He greatly needed air to clear his head and relax.

Once he was out of the manor, he let out a long-held breath. He wanted to go for a walk, but he knew he should not go too far from the safety of Roland's manor. He was grateful to Roland for bringing him back to life and full health, but he could not help but wonder if it was a mistake now. To take a life was a heavy burden, especially the life of a loved one. Aideen was his entire world, and now she was gone.

He leaned his back against the stone wall of the side of the manor, sliding to the ground in a fit of tears.

"Are you all right?" came a stranger's voice.

Caelum looked up to see the face of a man not much older than him.

"Why are you crying here in the dark, lad?"

Caelum sniffled, drying his eyes, and he stood back up. "It's nothing, I'm fine."

"Well, you shouldn't be out this late. There's a hunt going on," the stranger explained.

"A hunt?" Caelum asked, furrowing his brow.

"Yes, well, a demon hunt, actually. A demon killed a young girl. They believe an incubus stole her vitality and left her for dead," he continued.

Caelum looked at the man and burst into tears.

"Are you sure you're well? Did you know the girl?"

When Caelum did not answer, the stranger gently patted his shoulder. Caelum grabbed the man in a mournful hug, burying his face in the crook of the man's neck. The stranger made soothing noises as he patted Caelum's back. He pulled the crying boy away from him to look him in the eyes.

"There, there, lad. We'll find who did this and bring them to justice."

"It was me," Caelum whispered, sniffling still.

"What was that now?"

"I killed her," he mumbled, looking the man in eyes.

Again, he saw the white glow of his eyes reflected in someone else's. When he took a long whiff of the stranger, the man attempted to back away. He smelled of something bitter, but it was not entirely unappealing. The smell of his fear was delectable, however. Caelum grabbed the back of the man's head and kissed him hard. He could feel the man's erection against his own. The stranger stopped fighting him and relaxed into the kiss. Caelum broke the kiss, his lips hovering slightly over the man's as the ethereal strand of light passed from the man's mouth into his.

He was so hungry. He drained the stranger quickly, feeling the euphoric buzz of his vitality fill him. Before he knew it, the man was a brittle husk in his arms. Once the high of his lust was over, panic overwhelmed him. He frantically looked around for any witnesses, and was momentarily relieved to find none. They were alone, but he remembered the man said there was a hunt going on. He realized he needed to hide the body before anyone found them.

Caelum was grateful for the added strength his demonic blood provided, not that the stranger's husk weighed anything. Back in the comfort of his room,

Caelum broke down again. He had carelessly taken another life. The stranger's death left him feeling numb. He could tell no one what happened that night. Not even Roland. He was not supposed to be out, let alone tell anyone what he had done to Aideen. Control. He needed to learn control, but there was no one like him that could teach him. His previous illness got him banished from his coven, and they still would not take him back despite being cured of the disease. His coven thought he was cursed. With no family to help him, he was on his own.

CHAPTER 2

Several weeks had gone by since Aideen's death. Caelum had been sneaking out when he felt his demonic hunger pangs. He would still eat regular food, but he found that it only fed his stomach. His body craved the energy that came with being in contact with others. He lost his virginity to an unsuspecting neighbor that had been drawn to him. The gender of his victims did not matter to him now, so long as he could feed. Each person tasted different.

Though they tasted awful, vagrants were the easiest meals. With the uptake in missing persons, Caelum's guilt only grew. He knew what he was doing was wrong, but he could not help the impulse. It was biological, after all.

He fed discreetly, but his guilt and fear of being caught was tearing him apart. To cope with his warring emotions, he took up painting and sculpting. Roland had taken notice of his new hobbies and acknowledged his natural talent for the arts, but Caelum could see in the old man's eyes that he knew something was wrong.

"That is an interesting painting," came Roland's voice as he entered the makeshift studio he set up for Caelum.

Caelum frowned. "You don't like it?"

"I didn't say that," he replied. "It's just a bit dark, is all."

"Oh," he murmured, going back to his painting.

"Perhaps—and this is just a suggestion—you shouldn't paint where you're hiding the bodies," he grinned.

Caelum froze. He thought he was being careful. He made sure no one was around when he took a life. How did Roland find out?

"Calm down, boy," he chuckled. "You're secret's safe."

He turned to Roland. "How? How did you know?"

"I'm a god of death, remember? I can sense these things."

Caelum furrowed his brow. "But I thought you could only sense the deaths of those that have drowned."

"No, I can sense all deaths. I also have two familiars that can see all dead. Lux has been keeping an eye on you for me."

Caelum's eyes narrowed at Roland. "You've been having me followed?"

"You didn't think I'd let a young, untrained incubus go around eating people without some sort of supervision, did you?" he asked. "Your body count is getting rather high, but I commend your discretion."

Caelum frowned again. "So, what's going to happen now?"

"Well, you're going to have to learn control—better than you have been. You can't keep killing people, Caelum. It's dangerous. Not to mention, wrong."

"I know, and I've been trying, but once I get started, I can't stop myself."

"Hm, I see." Roland scratched at his stubble as he thought. Then it was as if something wonderful crossed his mind. His eyes lit up with whatever he was thinking. "Can you feed without intercourse?"

"Sometimes," he replied, bewildered. "But there has to be sexual energy present."

"Oh," he frowned. "Does it have to come from the person you're feeding on?"

"Yes, why?" Caelum asked in confusion.

"Hm..." he replied.

Caelum stared at Roland with a mix of confusion and concern. Roland's line of questions mortified him.

"Do you have to be in direct contact with whom you're feeding on?"

"Probably. I don't know," he sputtered.

16

"Hm..." he said again.

"Roland, what are you thinking?"

"Hm? Oh, I was thinking that you could feed from me," he replied absently.

Wide-eyed, Caelum responded, "I most certainly will not!"

Roland looked at him in confusion. "Why not? It's not like you can actually hurt me."

Caelum could not understand how Roland did not see the problem with his suggestion. "Because," he started. "I can't see you in a state of undress. You're like a father to me."

"I understand that, and I have no desire to see you in the nude, either. However, you can't keep going out killing people."

Caelum paled. "I don't know what else to do," he admitted.

"How would you feel about feeding on my energy while I'm with a woman?"

"But what of Airlia's memory?"

Roland's expression went serious, but it was not in anger. "I could never betray her memory. I don't want to be with anyone else, but I am responsible for you. You have to learn control, or at the very least how to feed in other ways," he explained.

A few moments of silence passed between them before Caelum spoke.

"All right. We'll try things your way, but what if it doesn't work? What if I can't feed without killing?"

Roland smiled wryly. "We'll worry about that another time." He gently placed his hand on Caelum's shoulder. "For now, we'll try feeding at a distance."

Caelum nodded solemnly. This was a gamble, but he knew something had to be done. He did not want to kill anymore.

The next day came far too fast for Caelum. He was unsure of how things were going to go, and there was some reluctance on Roland's end as well. Caelum knew that what was going to happen would eat at Roland. He did not know Airlia; she had died long before he had met Roland, but he knew how Roland felt about the woman. Her memory haunted Roland in the worst way. Roland was often sullen and withdrawn because he still grieved her loss.

When Roland offered to help him, it was almost out of character for him. And when he went out and came back with a woman he intended to bed, it shocked Caelum. He did not think Roland would actually forgo his celibacy for him. It was a touching thing to do. Roland may have saved his life, but he rarely ever showed he cared. Caelum knew he could only repay the kindness of Roland's sacrifices by living well, and at least trying harder to learn control.

"Caelum, come say hello," Roland beckoned.

The woman blushed hard when Caelum smiled at her.

"Oh, he's handsome. Is this your son?" she asked, not taking her eyes off Caelum.

"No," Roland said flatly. "But he is my ward."

"I see," she said in a breathy tone.

Caelum's cheeks flamed a bright red under the woman's inspection. He could smell her lust rising, and he was becoming uncomfortable with Roland standing there looking amused.

"Well, that'll be extra," she spoke, clearing her throat. "If I am to bed the two of you."

"Actually, you're just with me this evening," Roland corrected.

So, she was a courtesan. Caelum was not entirely sure at first, but she did smell of other men.

"Shall we get to it, then?" asked Roland.

The woman blinked wildly for a moment. She had been staring at Caelum again. She gave a curt nod as she took Roland's arm. Roland smiled at Caelum, then led the woman up the stairs to his room. Caelum followed shortly after. He was to sit outside the room and feed off the energy Roland projected. Still not sure if he could do it, he thought he would at least try.

He could hear them both through the closed door. Her moans were soft, delicate sounds that aroused Caelum. Whatever it was that Roland was doing to her, she was thoroughly enjoying herself. Caelum could feel his face warming with the noise. Whether it was from embarrassment or desire, he was not sure. It might as well have been both.

After a few minutes, Caelum felt his whole body heat up. The speed of their lovemaking increased, and Caelum was sure they were both close to climax. He could taste their lust in the air. He let out a strained growl as he fell to his knees, the tang of copper in his mouth as his fangs grew and pierced his lip.

There was a painful stinging at his temples as a pair of horns tore out of his skin and curved behind and around his ears. His fingers extended into long claws that dug into the floorboards with an awful screech. Caelum's eyes went wide at the sight of his black tipped talons, his breaths heavy with the onset of panic. He had never transformed before, and he was not sure what would happen next.

Panting hard, he bore his fangs at a passing servant. The young woman scampered away, clutching the linens she carried tight to her chest. He returned his attention to the closed bedroom door. There was a faint light emanating from it he had not noticed before. The light shimmered as it moved in a stream towards him. It smelled of a fresh spring and power. It smelled of Roland, a powerful dragon god. As the glittering, gossamer light entered him, he thought he would explode with its power. And he only wanted more.

"Well, that can't be good," came a familiar baritone.

Caelum looked up to see the worried faces of Luxor and Lynnox. The girl he had scared earlier must have alerted them to his current state.

"Look at him!" gasped Lynnox. "He's got horns!"

"I can see that. Perhaps we should get him put away before someone gets hurt?" Luxor offered.

Caelum growled at the pair of familiars as they cautiously approached him from the sides. He smiled malevolently as he stood, preparing himself for a fight. No one was taking him away from his meal. He felt electrified with power as it continued to flow into him.

"Sounds like Zaven's enjoyin' himself," Lynnox grumbled.

"He's not the only one," spoke Luxor, meeting Caelum's fierce, but euphoric, gaze. "I don't believe he's going to come peacefully."

"Bugger all!" Lynnox growled, readying herself for a fight.

Caelum took a step towards her, stumbling as he did so. He felt unsteady all of a sudden.

"Wonderful," sighed Luxor. "He's drunk."

Caelum swiped at Lynnox and fell back to his knees before collapsing and passing out.

When Caelum woke up, he felt strange all over. His body still tingled with the remnants of Roland's power. He had a vague memory of what happened before he collapsed and blacked out. He grimaced at what he did remember. When he moved to sit up, the room spun. Silently, he wondered if this was how a hangover felt since he did not consume alcohol.

The sound of the door opening caught his attention as he held his head. He made a mental note to have the loud squeak in the door dealt with later.

"Oh! Yer awake!" came Lynnox as she peeked her head in.

He winced and grumbled tiredly at her. She smiled warmly at him before going over to the window and drawing back the curtains. When he let out a sharp hiss, she closed them immediately.

"Sorry, love," she said, as she smiled apologetically.

Again, he grumbled in response.

Lynnox went over to him and pressed the back of her hand to his forehead and her other hand to hers. "Ya don't have a fever," she noted, checking him over.

He politely took her hands in his to stop her assault. "I'm fine, just a bit out of sorts, is all," he explained. "How long was I unconscious for?" he asked, releasing her.

"Not long," she replied, fussing with the skirt of her dress. "Just most of the day."

He sighed. "I'm sorry for last night. I don't know what came over me."

She gently patted his leg. "No need for all that. A god's power can be overwhelmin'. Ya didn't know what was gonna happen."

He knew she was right. In his recklessness, he had consumed a great deal of the vitality of a god, something unheard of among his kind as far as he knew. Gods were not known to live among mortals, and they most certainly did not share their life energy.

"Caelum, are ya well, love?"

He looked over to see her small, worried face. Smiling wryly, he said, "I think I need to rest."

She gave a small nod, patted his leg again, then turned to leave.

As he groggily shifted in his bed, Caelum's senses dulled, and his vision blurred. His room, once modest and comfortable, felt oppressive and stifling. He could still feel what remained of Roland's divine energy swirling within him. It was a chaotic mix of power and confusion. His body ached from the sheer intensity of what he absorbed. What concerned him most was that he wanted more. To feel the high of the surge of power again. Perhaps he would handle it differently the next time.

CHAPTER 3

O ver the course of the following weeks, Roland had taken more women to his bed, and Caelum fed off the projected energy from a distance. Each time, Caelum transformed, but he lost his aggression. However, the sexual high he got aroused by his own needs, and he escaped into the night and killed again. He was fortunate that he was in his demonic form the few times he had been spotted. Like a specter, he phased through the walls of his sleeping victims' homes and took their lives.

He had become increasingly addicted to Roland's energy, and his feeding windows grew shorter. Roland's energy was not lasting as long as they had hoped. Caelum was burning through it too quickly. Soon, Roland had to cut off his energy intake.

"But why?" Caelum asked. "I swear I'm starting to get the hang of my powers."

"Really? Because it seems to me that you've lost all control of them," Roland countered. "You're still killing, Caelum. No more."

At that, Caelum had no response. He held his hands in tight fists at his sides, doing his best to quell his growing rage. Roland was right, of course. He needed better control of his demonic nature.

It was late in the afternoon as he reclined against his favorite oak tree in the meadow just a short distance from where the manor stood. It was balmy outside, but that was typical of a summer day. That was when he saw her. She was picking wildflowers as she hummed peacefully to herself. He watched as she gathered a variety, oblivious to his presence. He had seen her around town before whenever he was out with Roland; she was always with her parents, but she appeared alone that day. It was never a good idea for a young lady to be without a chaperone. It was not proper, but who was he to judge? He was a killer, after all.

Caelum drew his knees to his chest with the thought. Still, he quietly watched the girl. She had creamy skin, flaxen hair, and soft brown eyes. The girl always seemed so cheerful when he saw her, but she appeared deep in thought as she continued to collect flowers in pinks and purples.

"They were her favorite colors," she spoke as she plucked another flower, not looking at him.

His eyes went wide. So, she had noticed him. He shrunk even more into himself, trying to be as small as possible.

She giggled. "You're a funny thing." She picked one last flower before walking over to him.

He recoiled from her outstretched hand, backing into the tree when she got closer.

She frowned at his reaction. "It's all right. I won't hurt you," she tried.

She must have thought him to be simple of mind. When he did not reply or move, she sighed and sat next to him instead. She sat the small bouquet down next to her, then turned to the frightened boy at her side.

"I'm Catherine. What's your name?" She smiled brightly as she mimicked him by tucking her knees into her chest.

Caelum knew he was being ridiculous, but he was absolutely terrified of being near people. "You shouldn't be near me," he murmured from behind his knees. "I'm a monster."

Again, she laughed. "You look like a nice boy to me," she replied. "You certainly don't look like a monster. Actually, you're quite handsome. And monsters aren't so scared of people."

Still, he sat frozen, staring at her with fearful eyes.

Her pink lips formed a line. His behavior seemed to vex her. She picked up one of the purple blossoms from her bundle and presented it to him. A peace offering, he supposed. When he did not accept it, she shrugged, then proceeded to remove the petals one by one, throwing them into the wind. They sat together in silence, her staring longingly out into the meadow, and him staring wildly at her.

After several agonizingly long moments, he relaxed just enough as she wiped a tear from her eye.

"Whose favorite colors?" he asked, barely above a whisper.

"Hm?" she replied.

"The flowers. Who are they for?"

"Oh!" She took another moment before responding. "My friend. She died suddenly a couple of weeks ago."

She sounded so sad. He wanted to ask what happened, but decided it was none of his business. "I'm sorry," he mumbled.

"Thank you," she smiled, her eyes shining with unshed tears.

He looked out to see that the sun was setting. Quickly, he scrambled to his feet. Everything in him was telling him to get back to the manor, but he did not want to leave her alone at dusk. He knew he was not the only monster in the area that preyed on young girls. So, he let go of his fear and offered her his hand to help her up.

"It's not safe for a young lady to be out alone at this hour," he said. "Please, allow me to escort you home."

She blinked wildly up at him for a moment, before scrubbing her eyes free from the tears. "But I don't even know your name."

He knitted his brow in confusion, then remembered he never told her his name. "My apologies. My name is Caelum," he replied, still offering his hand.

She smiled and took hold of his outstretched hand, allowing him to pull her to her feet. When he pulled her up, she stumbled into his arms. They both turned bright red, and he steadied her, bending down to retrieve her flowers, but she had the same idea, and their heads connected with a muted clunk. They laughed as they rubbed their aching skulls, and he handed her the flowers.

Again, she smiled, still blushing. "Thank you."

He felt his cheeks burn, and he bashfully turned his gaze away, clearing his throat. "We should get go—" he started to say, but her soft lips pressed against his still burning cheek, cutting him off.

When he turned in surprise to face her, their lips touched. They once again turned the hue of red, both avoiding the other's eyes.

When he turned back to her, she brazenly threw herself into his arms and kissed him before he could protest. His eyes went wide in disbelief, but he melted into the kiss, wrapping his arms around her waist. After a few precious moments, he broke their kiss. His mouth hovered over hers, and he could feel his body pull the ethereal light from within her. A voice at the back of his mind screamed at him to stop, but he found he could not. Soon, the light in her went out and filled him, and all that remained was a gray husk, with dead, sunken eyes staring at him. Tears ran down his face in mournful torrents as he howled into the encroaching darkness.

He bolted upright in a cold sweat, his breathing coming out in panicked bursts. Clutching his chest, he attempted to calm himself. He realized he was dreaming again, remembering that Catherine had died by his hands years ago.

Once his breathing evened out and his heart stopped trying to escape the confines of his chest, he noticed he was not at home in his bed. He was outside, of all places, and it was dark. He gave his eyes another moment to adjust to the dark as he felt around. The frozen chill of ice ran down his spine when his hand touched what felt like parchment wrapped around something slender and solid. His eyes moved slowly to where his hand rested, and he snatched his hand away as if he had been burned. A scream caught in his throat, and he hastened away from the husk that lay on the ground. A pale yellow dress hung loose around the skeletal remains of a woman with dark, brittle hair he did not recognize. Frantically, he got to his feet and looked around. It was late and no one else was around.

The last thing he remembered was going to bed after dinner. He had been doing his best to abstain from feeding, and he always made sure he was secured to his bed with heavy chains after he woke up outside one too many times with dirt all over his hands and clothes. This time, he remained with the body. As quickly as he could, he ran back to the safety of the manor. He was too frightened to hide the body this time. Another report of an incubus attack would be made. He was sure of it.

CHAPTER 4

"Well, why didn't you stop him?" Roland fussed.

"Because he would have fought me, and the fight would have brought unwanted attention," replied Luxor. "And I can't follow him everywhere when he can pass through walls."

"Then you should have told me," Roland countered.

Caelum stood and watched the exchange. Chains were not enough to stop him, and Luxor could only do so much. Especially while he was in his feline form. Even if he had turned back into his human form, there was no guarantee he could subdue Caelum while he was in his demonic form. Caelum felt like a blight on his savior's home.

It was decided. He would use the money he earned from selling his art and take his chances on his own in London. It was his plan with Aideen all those years ago. He reflexively put his hand over his heart, squeezing his chest. Thinking of Aideen still hurt. Her memory like a fresh wound. Compounded with the faces of his countless victims, he was a tightly wound ball of guilt. He did not want Roland to bear any blame for the deaths he caused.

As Roland and Luxor continued to argue over him, Caelum turned to leave. He needed to pack.

"Caelum?" came Roland. He jogged to remove the distance between them. "You didn't hear all that, did you?"

"It's all right. You've been good to me these last eleven years. It's time I moved on and got out of your hair," he admitted solemnly.

"You know you don't have to. We'll figure things out."

"There's nothing to figure out, Roland," Caelum started. "I can't keep putting you and others at risk."

"But it's not safe for you out there," Roland pleaded.

"It's not safe for me here, either," he countered. "I'm a grown man now. I can take care of myself."

"You're twenty-one, boy," Roland scoffed. "You are far from grown."

"Well, not compared to a god, I'm not! But as a mortal, I am an adult."

A moment of silence passed between them as they stared at one another. Caelum realized he was just as tall as Roland now, and almost as broad. The look in Roland's sad brown eyes said he saw Caelum was no longer a child, at least not in the physical sense.

Caelum smiled. "I'll be all right, old man."

Roland sighed. "If it's what you want, I won't stop you. Just keep your head down and stay safe." He placed both his hands on Caelum's shoulders. "And promise me you'll get control."

Caelum frowned. "I'll do my best," he said after a moment.

Roland gave Caelum's shoulders a light, paternal squeeze. "You had better." He lightly patted his face, then turned to leave. "Go do great things with the life I've returned to you."

The move to London was bittersweet. Caelum said his goodbyes. Lynnox cried, of course, and he was on his way. He had enough saved to purchase a small home on the outskirts of town. Which suited him just fine. He would spend his days painting or sculpting, and his nights hunting. He stuck to the seedy parts of London, and only took vagrants and lone prostitutes as lovers. Their flavor disgusted him, and their energy did not last him for more than a day or two. He tried to find non-humans to feed on for their resilience, hoping it would help him with his control, but they were usually wary of him. His demonic blood must have given off a particular scent, he assumed.

He wiped his brow of sweat after he tossed the shovel out of the hole. He hopped out shortly after. Dusting himself off, he inspected the depth of the freshly dug hole, then turned his attention to the husk down at his side. He sighed as he bent to heave the remains of a homeless beggar into the hole. It was easy enough to seduce him. He simply had to promise him a meal and a good time. He did not even bother to learn the man's name. It never did him any good to learn their names. Their faces haunted him all the same.

As he shoveled the dirt back into the hole, he looked around the wooded area. There was not much around and he was grateful for that, but there were many lumps of disturbed earth. Perhaps he should consider a different method of disposal, he thought to himself. Roland would be most disappointed with him. He turned quickly when he heard the crunching of twigs on the ground. He let out a sigh of relief when he saw what it was. A small black cat with a perfect white teardrop on his head.

Putting the shovel down, he frowned at the furry intruder. "I swear I'm trying to do better. There's no need for you to keep watch over me," he grumbled. "I'm fine."

The Nakaru meowed his disagreement at him, then vanished in a puff of smoke.

Again, Caelum sighed. He did not believe he was fine either. At least his art career was starting to go somewhere. He certainly was not lacking in inspiration. Still, his lack of control would soon get him caught. He hoped that the energy would satisfy him for the next day or so. That gave him some time to find others like him to help. Until then, he would get some much needed rest.

He finished filling the hole and patted the earth down as best he could, then ventured back home for the night. It would be dawn soon and he had a lot to do in a short amount of time.

CHAPTER 5

The city was busy that evening. Caelum did not understand why. There were no festivals going on or dignitaries visiting that he knew of. Still, the populace seemed in good spirits despite the poverty and murders he was not involved in. Though he knew the ones he committed made them worry as well. However, that was how things were in the lower part of London. He stayed clear of the high-class part, especially at night, only going there to sell his art and buy supplies. Lower London was where he was most at ease. Where he felt he belonged. It reminded him of where he died in Wales and where he was resurrected. Among the dirt and grime of the dregs of society was the perfect place for him to start a new life.

"Hey there, handsome. Lookin' for a nice place to warm your cock?" offered a raspy female voice. "I bet I'd fit like a glove."

The haggard–looking woman had startled him out of his thoughts as she sucked on a cigarette, blowing smoke at him.

"Not tonight," he replied, doing his best to not appear disgusted.

She flicked the remnant of her cigarette to the ground, making a tsking sound as she ground it out under her boot. "Your loss, wanker," she spat, then sauntered off in the opposite direction.

Perhaps he did not belong as much as he originally thought.

"Get out, you filthy mongrel!" came a loud, harsh voice of a man. "And don't show your face here again!"

Caelum rounded the corner in time to see a rather large, scruffy young man being tossed out of a brothel Caelum was familiar with.

"Your kind ain't welcome here," he bellowed as he slammed the door.

The man that had been thrown out staggered back to his feet and spat on the ground. He smelled wild and untamed, but most strongly of alcohol.

"What're you starin' at, pretty boy?" he growled as he wiped drool and dirt from his face.

Under the torch light, Caelum could see the man had tousled, shaggy black hair that rested on his broad shoulders. His hair framed a firm jaw and blue eyes darkened by intoxication. His skin was a dark olive color over a lean, muscular body. He towered over Caelum, and he was beautiful in his rugged appearance.

"I said: what're you starin' at?" he asked again, this time standing painfully close.

Caelum swallowed hard. Now that he was so close, Caelum could see the wolf's fangs, and he finally recognized the wild, earthy scent. He was not prepared for a fight. Especially not with a werewolf.

The wolf furrowed his brow. "Are you deaf or a half-wit?"

"I'm sorry," Caelum spoke at last, shaking his head. "I didn't mean any offense."

"Whatever," he grumbled, pushing past Caelum. "Get outta my way, runt."

Caelum watched as he drunkenly stalked away. The wolf looked to be around his age and smelled powerful. From the looks of him, he had been sleeping on the streets for a short while. The wolf's clothes were tattered, worn, and filthy. Of course, he was not welcomed in a brothel.

He did not smell of a pack, and no one else was with him. He was likely a lone wolf, and he would make an excellent meal. Provided he could get past the foul assortment of smells.

He followed the wolf as he continued to stumble away.

"Why are you following me, little man?" he growled, snatching a liquor bottle from another drunk on the street as he continued his angry jaunt.

Caelum avoided the bottle when it hit the ground. Carelessly tossed aside once it served its purpose. He continued to follow the wolf at a short distance, waiting for the right opportunity.

"If you're looking for easy money, you're followin' the wrong man," he growled, coming to a halt.

He turned, baring his fangs. Caelum stopped where he was and held his hands up.

"I swear, I mean you no harm," said Caelum.

"Then why are you followin' me?"

"I was just curious about you, that's all," he replied, putting his hands down slowly.

"Well, out with it," he said after a moment.

Caelum let out a held breath. He was curious about the wolf, but he was, so far, hostile. He was thinking he may not be worth the trouble. "I was wondering where the rest of your pack was? You don't seem... well cared for."

"What business is it of yours?" he snarled.

"I'm sorry. I didn't mean to upset you," Caelum said, holding his hands out as if to stop the angry wolf from charging.

The wolf's lip curled up in a sneer. Then he turned to walk away again.

Caelum felt somewhat sorry for him. A lone wolf did not last long without the support of their pack. They were either killed by another pack for being in their territory or they starved. A werewolf was not much of a threat on their own. Though he still looked strong, he also seemed lonely.

He shook his head to clear the thoughts of his own loneliness. That was not important. He needed to feed his demon. He would be doing the wolf a favor, putting him out of his misery. So, he jogged to catch up to him.

"Stay away from me, or I'll eat you," the wolf growled, still walking away.

"It's dangerous to be out here on your own," Caelum spoke.

"I'm doin' just fine on my own."

"Perhaps I can offer you a hot meal and a warm place to lay your head," Caelum tried.

At that, the wolf stopped again, turning to face Caelum. "What's it to you if I'm out on my own? You some kinda missionary?"

"Nothing of the sort."

"Then what do you get outta helpin' me?"

"Someone to share a meal with?"

The wolf narrowed his eyes. "You sure you're not a missionary?"

"My place isn't far. Just outside of the city."

Caelum waited patiently for the wolf's response.

"Do you know why I got tossed from that brothel?"

The question caught Caelum off guard. He had already made up his mind why he was thrown out. He did not think it was something up for discussion. Bewildered, he shook his head in response.

"Because," he started, walking up to Caelum.

He was painfully close again, and Caelum found it difficult to hide his apprehension or his growing desire.

"I dared to want another man," he finished, looking Caelum square in the eyes. "Do you understand now?"

Caelum gulped, then nodded. "I'm Caelum," he said, taking a step back and offering his hand.

A knowing smirk crept up on the wolf's full lips as he took Caelum's hand. "Ariel."

The walk back to Caelum's home was not terribly long, but it was not short either. They walked in silence, but it was deafening to Caelum. He had to remind himself that he could not get to know Ariel. Though he wanted to know why he was kicked out of his pack as well. No, getting to know his food was never the best course of action. It only added to the guilt he already had for treating them like cattle, but it was the only way to reconcile taking a life. Even if he did not mean to do it.

"You're awfully quiet, pretty boy. Not having second thoughts, are you?" Ariel inquired.

"Hm?" Caelum asked, disturbed from his thoughts. "Oh, no. Just thinking it will be nice to have company."

Ariel scoffed at that. "We're not friends. I just need a place to stay for the night and food in my belly," he grumbled.

"Right," Caelum started. "Of course."

Ariel tossed another bottle to the ground he had snatched from another man drunk on the street they had passed on their way out of the city. At least there would be one less person littering the streets with broken glass, Caelum thought to himself.

Caelum had been accustomed to preparing his own meals while living with Roland. He did not have to do it, but he insisted on it. Though he did not prepare his meals all the time, he was proficient at it. It was a strange thing making a meal for someone else.

Ariel devoured his food like the starving wolf he was, and Caelum did his best to eat his without gagging from watching Ariel. He was not expecting a werewolf to behave like a refined gentleman, especially a homeless one, but he could have had some manners, at the very least.

"Pardon me," he said after releasing a belch loud enough for the gods to hear. He smiled with his fangs as he patted his full belly. "That was delicious."

Perhaps this was a mistake. Caelum found that he no longer had an appetite for wolf energy. Ariel's entire demeanor was disgusting and off-putting, but he knew he had to feed his demon or risk killing indiscriminately and exposing himself.

So, he decided to get to know the wolf, hoping it would take his mind off his abhorrent behavior. "Why don't you tell me why you were let go from your pack?" he asked, putting his utensils down.

"I told you already. It's none of your business," Ariel replied nonchalantly as he reclined in his chair. He picked a sliver of meat from his teeth with an extended claw from his little finger.

"Well, it is my business, actually," he countered. "I want to make sure I didn't invite a killer into my home."

Ariel regarded him thoughtfully. He had a look of suspicion in his eyes, leaving Caelum to wonder if his powerful sense of smell could tell what he was. He hoped that Ariel's mild inebriation dulled his senses.

"I was 'let go' because I loved the wrong wolf," he grumbled solemnly.

"Did your lover not think to join you in exile?"

"No," he said flatly. "He was the pack leader's only son and heir."

"I see," said Caelum. "That doesn't seem like such a thing worthy of exile."

"It wasn't. I challenged the alpha and won."

"But I don't understand."

"I refused to kill my love's father. They were all they had left," he explained. "I was banished for showing mercy."

"Oh, I'm sorry to hear that."

"There's nothing to be sorry for."

"But you were punished for doing the right thing."

Ariel chuckled. "Yes, and I'd do it again."

"What of your lover? Did he have nothing to say on the matter?"

"He did." Ariel frowned at that. "He did the right thing by not coming with me," he replied after a moment. "He's most likely mated to the daughter of another pack leader by now. An alliance was what his father wanted, and what the pack needed."

Caelum silently nodded. Hearing Ariel's story made him uneasy about what he brought him to his home for. He knew it would. Ariel had lost his love as well. He was a kindred spirit, in a way. At least he would have a chance to love again. After taking Aideen's life, Caelum knew he could never. It was not worth the risk. That settled things. He would let Ariel go. He would find another meal.

"Are you all right?" Ariel asked, his brow furrowed when Caelum doubled over in pain.

"I'm fine," he growled out. "You should leave."

"You don't look fine."

"Stay back," he shouted when Ariel got too close.

"Shit! You're an incubus!"

"Yes, please don't tell anyone," he pleaded. It was all he could do to stave off his transformation. Ariel's alpha energy smelled absolutely delectable.

"When was the last time you fed?"

Was that concern he was hearing? "A few days," he groaned. "If you value your life, you will leave."

"No, I won't leave you like this," he replied. "If anyone catches you out hunting like this, you'll be killed."

"Please, I don't want to hurt you!"

"You won't, I won't let you. I owe you for the meal and bed," he explained. "Let me help you."

"I don't have control," he cried. "I've killed so many already."

"Oh," Ariel said in shock. "Well, then let me help you."

Caelum looked up into Ariel's clear blue eyes. There was some apprehension, but there was also determination. "All right," he half whispered.

He allowed Ariel to help him as he directed him to his bedroom. It took everything in him not to take

Ariel the moment he touched him. Perhaps he had more control than he thought.

All his hard-fought control was gone when they got to his room and Ariel stripped out of his clothing. He had a well cut, muscular body. From his chest, to his abdomen, to the sinful V that led to an impressive cock. Caelum was suddenly self-conscious of his own body.

"I appreciate the compliment," Ariel said, a smirk creeping up his face when he caught Caelum staring.

Before Caelum could respond, Ariel surged forward, his mouth crashing into his in a heated kiss. Caelum responded to Ariel's passion almost instantly, his hands finding Ariel's waist and pulling him flush against him. Ariel's kiss was fierce, like he was starving for contact. Desperate and consuming. It was intoxicating. His taste, the earthy scent of him, the heat of his hard body.

Ariel broke their kiss, the haze of lust in his eyes. "Here, let me," he said as he undressed Caelum.

Once Caelum was void of all clothing, Ariel took a moment to look him over. Caelum flushed red under the inspection. He was not bad to look at. He was pale and toned, but he was not built like Ariel. Ariel smiled at him, then dropped to his knees. The bold wolf looked up at Caelum through hooded eyes, silently seeking permission as he took hold of Caelum's girthy cock. Caelum swallowed hard as he nodded his consent, biting his lip in anticipation.

A low growl erupted from Ariel, and then his mouth was on the head of Caelum's hard shaft. Caelum hissed at the sensation of the warm, wet cavern of Ariel's mouth. Ariel's tongue massaged the head of Caelum's prick, then he slowly ran his tongue from base to crown. Caelum groaned, his blue-green eyes clenched shut. Ariel lapped the translucent bead that leaked from the slit of the head, almost growling at the saltiness that prickled his tongue.

Caelum's hand found its way into Ariel's hair, his fingers tightening around his locks to guide his head to take more of him into his mouth. Ariel's lips strained around Caelum's mass, his tongue swirling around the flare of his head. Each time he did, light traces of his seed coated his tongue, his own cock twitching with need. It was almost like a mirror of how Caelum's legs trembled the closer he got to release, barely able to continue standing on his own.

Ariel's strokes sped up as Caelum's moans urged him on. Caelum gasped, his hips jerking forward, and his fingers tight in Ariel's hair. He held him in place as he released the warm streams of his seed into Ariel's waiting mouth. And he greedily swallowed every drop, Caelum's partially erect cock still seated in his mouth.

Caelum looked down at Ariel after he released him, both panting. He wiped the semen from the corner of Ariel's mouth with his thumb, then helped him to his feet. His eyes darkened with greater lust when Ariel's still hard member touched his, his own erection coming alive again with the contact. Their lips met again, and Caelum walked Ariel backwards to his bed. He pushed the wolf down, and before he could protest, he lifted his legs, then positioned himself at his entrance. He plunged himself into the dark depths of Ariel's rear, a look of elation on his lust-drunk face as he reveled in the tightness of him. Ariel grunted at the rough intrusion, but Caelum was not concerned. He was far too enthralled by Ariel's warmth.

His thrusts were hard and fast as Ariel writhed beneath him. Soon, he was close to climax again. He could feel Ariel's life energy pouring into him as he pumped almost ruthlessly into him. Suddenly, he felt the firm grip of Ariel's large hands around his throat, breaking the spell of his lust as he was being deprived of oxygen. He stopped his thrusting as he tried to remove Ariel's hands from his throat. When he could focus again, he saw the wild, feral look on Ariel's face as his breathing was labored again. Caelum was released from Ariel's hold when he stopped pulling on his life force. After he pulled out of him, Ariel collapsed into unconsciousness. Caelum had taken enough of the wolf's energy to satisfy his demonic need. He checked Ariel for a pulse, and was relieved to find one. Though he buzzed with Ariel's delicious energy, he found that he, too, was exhausted. He climbed into the bed and passed out next to Ariel.

CHAPTER 6

Caelum found himself walking down a dimly lit, seemingly endless corridor. He saw various paintings on the walls, which he recognized as his own, but they were distorted and twisted. As he continued down the corridor, he heard faint whispers and cries, and they grew louder with each step he took forward.

Suddenly, the corridor opened into a vast, dark room. In the center of the room was a single torch light illuminating a figure lying on the ground. The flames of the light flickered and danced, creating haunting shadows. As Caelum approached the figure, he recognized it as one of his victims. Their eyes were fixed open wide, staring blankly, their face contorted in agonized pain.

Caelum tried to speak. He wanted to apologize, but the words caught in his throat. Instead, the room filled with echoes of his voice, reciting the names of all the people he had unintentionally killed. Each name acted as a weight pressing down on him, making it hard for him to breathe.

Panicked, his powers flared up. Shadows swirled around him, and he suddenly felt an overwhelming urge to feed. He was desperate to resist, but the more he fought it, the stronger the urge became, until it consumed him.

He woke up in a cold sweat, his heart still pounding in his ears, the faces of his victims seared in his mind. Caelum was left feeling isolated and terrified of his demonic blood. The nightmare served to reinforce his fear of getting close to others. However, when he turned to his side, there, sleeping soundly, was Ariel. The wolf had shown no fear of his nature and did what he could to appease his demonic hunger. And all without dying. Caelum had fed his demon, and his partner survived.

He stared at the sleeping wolf in disbelief. Then he remembered why Ariel was still alive. Had Ariel not stopped him, Caelum would have had another husk to bury. But Caelum had hope still. If he could keep Ariel close, he would not have to kill again. The only issue he saw was letting his victims go. They would undoubtedly inform the authorities of his actions, and he would be executed. There had to be a way to prevent that from happening.

"Your face will stay that way if you don't fix it," came a tired, gravelly voice.

Caelum looked to his side and saw that Ariel was awake.

"That look isn't much better," he grumbled, when Caelum's face turned to an apologetic expression.

"But I lured you here with the promise of food and a warm bed, and nearly killed you," he replied.

"Yes, but you also tried to warn me. You are not at fault for my stubbornness," he countered, placing his hands behind his head.

"You're right, but had you been a weaker man, I would have another body to dispose of," he retorted.

"Fair enough. Why don't you have control? Don't you have a coven to teach you?"

Caelum sighed, hanging his head. "No, I was orphaned before I came into my powers."

"Ah, so you survived an extermination?"

"Wrong again. I was cast out for having a disease that's deadly to other incubi," he explained. "I died eleven years ago from it."

At that, Ariel sat up. "Then how are you still here?"

Caelum grimaced. He was not sure how to explain that a god of death had given him a second life. More importantly, he was not sure if he should have. "It's complicated, I'm afraid," he decided.

Ariel raised a suspicious brow, but relented. "Then how have you survived this long on your own?"

"Pure, dumb luck, I suppose," he chuckled nervously. "I honestly just keep to myself until I need to feed or sell my art."

"Oh, so you're an artist!"

"Something like that," he blushed. "I mostly paint landscapes, and I occasionally am asked to do a portrait. I also sculpt."

"I see. So, you're alone then?"

"Yes, it's better that way," he admitted.

"It's dangerous that way. You need someone to help you."

Caelum regarded Ariel thoughtfully for a moment. The wolf was right; it was dangerous for him to be on his own, but he had been just fine until then.

"What's goin' on in that pretty head of yours?" Ariel asked.

"I was thinking you may be right, but I can't ask anyone to help me. I don't trust myself."

"Then trust that I know what I'm doin'," he offered. "You give me a place to lay my head, and I'll help you learn control."

Caelum took a few moments to think on his offer. It was what he wanted, to keep Ariel close, but he could not feed on him too often. Prolonged feedings invited madness, and Caelum did not want that for Ariel. Madness always led to death.

"I'll take your offer, but know that I cannot feed solely on you."

"I understand. You prefer the company of women."

"Mainly, yes, but I have had male lovers as well. That's just how my people are."

"All right, then I'll help you hunt and make sure they leave alive."

"And how do you propose we do that?" Caelum asked, genuinely curious. "I prefer to feed in private."

"Until you can control yourself, that stops," he replied sternly.

Caelum narrowed his eyes. "I thought we weren't friends."

"After last night, we are now," Ariel chuckled. "I've never been fucked like that before. Not sure how I feel about it. My ass hurts, by the way."

"I'm sure it does," Caelum laughed. "And I will never know that pain. Do we have an understanding?" he asked, his expression darkening.

"And if I don't agree?" Ariel challenged.

"Then you will be out on your ass again. Sore or not."

Ariel took a few moments to think as he glared at Caelum, who showed no fear of him, and glared right back.

He let out a sigh. "Fine, have it your way, but go easy on me next time," he relented. "Joshua always said it felt good, but how things went last night was not what I was expectin'."

"Yes, sorry about that. I'm usually quite gentle, but there was something about your energy that overwhelmed me." He looked away, feeling shame for his lack of control.

"Hey, it's all right. You'll get control in no time with my help."

Caelum furrowed his brow. "Have you trained many incubi before?"

"No, you're my first. But how hard can it be?" Ariel shrugged.

Caelum sighed in frustration, but before he could speak again, Ariel grabbed and kissed him passionately.

He momentarily broke their kiss and said, "Maybe feedin' your demon more often might overwhelm you less." He kissed Caelum again before he could argue.

Caelum gave into his desire, and they had sex again that morning. Ariel had to once again stop Caelum from taking too much of his energy, but he knew it was something they had to work on together.

As the days passed, Caelum and Ariel became better acquainted with one another. With Ariel's help, Caelum soon learned better control during his feedings. The first few times did not go well, even with Ariel keeping watch, but he learned with more frequent feedings he was not losing himself in the lust as often. To prevent the survivors from reporting him, Caelum found a witch that gave him a powder to help them forget the experience. It also helped that Ariel took the sleeping victims somewhere else to wake up.

Soon, Caelum could feed without his partner noticing. He realized that Ariel's desire for men often led to him being thrown out of brothels and other places. Though, he eventually found the hidden den of an all-male brothel deep within the bowels of the city. It catered to the supernatural, and he even had a favorite boy he would visit whenever Caelum was busy and did not need to feed. He would take on odd jobs to fund his baser needs.

Caelum had wished there was a place where people could openly indulge in their taboo interests without judgement. Then it struck him that he could create such a place, where courtesans could cater to their specific interests and desires. They would be like dolls he could fashion into whatever a person desired.

"Dolls?" Ariel asked, bewildered by the idea when Caelum told him of it. "Are you mad?"

"Why is it such a strange thing? Don't you want to be fucked by someone other than me? And not be tossed out for it?"

Ariel stared at Caelum with an expression that was a mix of amusement and doubt.

Caelum glared back at him. "You don't think it could work, do you?"

"I didn't say that, but I know you're daft enough to pull it off. It helps that you're pretty, too," he laughed. "But I don't know about callin' them Doll Houses."

"Why not? Brothels and bordellos are so boring."

"I suppose so," he replied, still laughing and shaking his head.

"Say what you will, but it's a good idea. There are many that live in the shadows that would enjoy my Dolls."

"All right, I'll help you in your business venture. I'll even be your first Doll."

Caelum gave him a dubious look.

"What? I think it's a good idea. You'd have a safe place to feed, and I'd make one hell of a Doll for the right price," he grinned.

Caelum shut his eyes and sighed. He would have his work cut out for him, trying to train the almost savage wolf. Perhaps there were those out there that liked what Ariel exuded.

Over the following weeks, the two of them got to work formulating plans for their business. Ariel agreed to model for Caelum to help earn more money faster so they could purchase the building they needed.

Once they had the building they wanted, they went about their recruiting process for potential Dolls and the needed security. The people they talked to thought it was a strange idea for a brothel and rejected their offer. Caelum noticed there had been some noted fear behind some of the rejections. Ariel smelled it, too.

While they continued their search for prostitutes that were not afraid to work with them, they noticed there had been a surge in missing persons of the supernatural variety. Caelum thought he had chosen his victims poorly, and that he would soon be discovered, but none of the missing people were his victims. There had also been an uptake in brutal slayings of supernatural beings. Some whispered of fanatical hunters or even cults at work. There was one hunter's name that was mentioned, but Caelum thought little of it.

Ariel suggested they not stay out late anymore because of the killings. It worried Caelum that Ariel did not believe in his own strength to fend off a hunter. But he considered the number of large, powerful creatures that were killed for parts, and agreed to not be out late. Though he noticed the humans were not concerned, and the authorities were doing nothing about the murders. He was not the least bit surprised by their inaction. They would only get involved if humans or someone important wound up dead.

CHAPTER 7

Caelum and Ariel were at a loss for how to get more people interested in the making of their Doll House. They thought two attractive men would be enough to draw others in, but they were wrong. To make matters worse, they heard rumors and whispers about them in a not-so-flattering light. Feeling tired and defeated, they did their sulking in a local tavern.

"I don't understand what we're doing wrong," spoke Caelum.

Ariel grumbled into his drink in response.

Caelum narrowed his eyes at him. "That is extraordinarily unhelpful, Ariel."

"I still think we should go to the rich part of town for help. That's where the money and the freaks are," Ariel replied as he downed his pint and signaled to the barkeep for another.

"That's your fourth pint, Ariel. Don't you think you've had enough?" asked Caelum.

Ariel shot him a nasty glare, then snatched the tankard of ale from the barmaid that brought it to him.

Caelum gave the girl an apologetic look before she huffed away. Before he could scold Ariel on his behavior, the door of the tavern swung open. In stepped a beautiful, feral-looking woman with brown, lightly spotted skin and long, flowing dark hair that fell in loose waves down her back. She sauntered seductively past their table, her long, spotted tail swaying gracefully behind her. She had a small, lithe body made for speed and agility. Caelum recognized her as a Nevala, a warrior built for dragon slaying. Sadly, there were no more Andr for her kind to fight.

The woman was bold and vivacious, pushing a sleeping drunk off the bar stool she wanted. He did not protest, but merely made himself comfortable on the floor. She perched herself on the stool, turning to face the full room of spectators, and smiled broadly, bearing her upper and lower canines as she leaned back. She rested her elbows on the bar and crossed her long legs, getting more than a few whistles and howls from her captive audience. Even Ariel was entranced by her.

"Who wants to buy the lady a pint?" she asked the room, slurring her words slightly.

The room erupted in laughter when she tried to straighten up and fell unceremoniously on her arse. It had been in Caelum's experience that felines always landed on their feet. That was not the case for the young Nevala.

She got to her feet, screaming and yelling obscenities. It was obvious now she had been drinking before she arrived. When someone tried to help her, she hissed at them. She started carrying on about a hunter taking her mate from her, and how she needed to find and kill them. She pleaded for anyone to help her, tears glistening in her honey brown eyes, but no one answered the call. Instead, they went back to their drinks and conversations.

When she saw no one would help her, she screamed and cursed as she threw bar stools, chairs, and tables. Two large men took her by the arms and dragged her kicking and screaming out of the place. She had lost her mate, and at such a young age. Caelum knew Nevala mated for life, and she would not likely take another. He saw the opportunity to get a potential Doll.

"No," Ariel grumbled. He could see the wheels turning in Caelum's mind as his eyes followed the woman out the door. "She just lost her mate, and she's far too wild."

"But she's gorgeous, and she seems like she could use a friend or two."

"No," Ariel said again.

"She's going to have needs that will need to be met. I say we give it a shot," Caelum tried excitedly.

"Absolutely not." Ariel glared over his pint.

Caelum grinned. "I bet if we offer to help her find this hunter, she'd be willing to join our merry band."

Ariel sighed. "You're not gonna let this go, are you?"

Caelum shook his head as he smiled.

Ariel let out an exasperated sigh before downing the rest of his drink. Reluctantly, he got up, and with a tired look in his eyes, "Let's go fetch her, then."

Caelum jumped up out of his seat, then followed Ariel out the door. When they were outside, the two men that escorted the Nevala out brushed past them roughly.

"Calm yourself," Caelum warned lightly when Ariel growled in response to the rude behavior.

The Nevala was getting up from the ground and dusting herself off when they got to her.

"And what the hell do you two want?" she asked, pulling bits of debris from her hair.

"We've come to make you an offer," said Caelum.

She narrowed her eyes at them. "I think not," she scoffed, then turned to walk away.

"Please, it's a splendid—"

The sound of him hitting the ground cut his words short. She had put him down hard and fast when he reached for her. Ariel snickered.

"Never touch me again," she hissed, her golden-brown eyes ablaze with fury.

She took a defensive stance when Ariel stepped forward. He held up his hands in surrender as he moved to Caelum's side.

"We only came to offer our help," he said, pulling Caelum to his feet. "We mean you no ill will."

She eyed them with an air of suspicion. "Why would I want help from such a weak demon and a mongrel wolf?"

At that, Ariel took offense, and Caelum had to hold him back when he heard the rumble of Ariel's growl.

"Well, you seemed desperate back there," Caelum said, pointing at the tavern. "We didn't think you would be so picky about what help was offered."

"All right, I'll bite. What'll it cost me?"

Ariel gave Caelum a warning glance, and Caelum understood the meaning. He needed to choose his words more wisely. So, he carefully told her about what they wanted to achieve, and what role they would each play. He omitted the part about him being an incubus in case she mistook him for a cambion of some variety, and he disclosed his relationship with Ariel. Much to Ariel's dismay.

"I would have never guessed from looking at him, but now I understand why you'd want such a place," she laughed. "But are you sure about calling it a Doll House?"

Again, Ariel snickered and received a nasty look from Caelum for it.

"How cute, a lover's spat," she giggled.

Ariel cleared his throat and straightened up. Caelum rolled his eyes at the posturing, then returned his attention to the Nevala.

"So, is it a deal?" he asked. "Will you help us?"

She mulled over his proposition for a few moments before giving her answer. "I suppose I could, but only after I have that hunter's heart in my hand."

"I will personally see to it."

"Then we have an accord," she said, holding out her hand.

"My name is Caelum," he replied, shaking her hand. "And the silent brute at my side is Ariel."

"Charlotte," she smiled.

The trio agreed to meet the following evening to discuss how they planned to find the hunter that killed her mate. They realized they needed to gather a lot of information, so they called it a night to get the rest they required. Caelum had a lightness in his step as he and Ariel traveled home. He now had two Dolls for his House. He even had control over his feedings. Things were looking better and better for him in his new life. He would need to report his progress and ambitions to Roland when he got the chance.

Caelum and Ariel met Charlotte at a different tavern late that afternoon. Charlotte had told them all she could remember about her mate's last hunt. He had told her that others of their kind had gone missing, only to wind up dead. Their bodies mangled. They had suspected a human hunter of the crimes because of the way the lost were found. The killings were ritualistic, with no respect shown to the victim. A hunter that used dark magic was who they were looking for.

It was not much to go on, but Nevala were not the only group of supernatural creatures that were victims of the ritualistic killings. This had been happening sporadically for over a year, and always four at a time. They asked around for any information, and Caelum noted the fear and apprehension of those they asked. They would get nothing with how they were asking. A change in tactics was needed. So, despite Ariel's reluctance, they split up, agreeing to meet back at the tavern at nightfall. Caelum hoped Charlotte would get more information on her own, provided she kept her emotions in check and stayed sober.

When the trio reconvened at the tavern, Ariel and Charlotte had sullen looks on their faces. Caelum assumed they had gotten the same reaction from when they traveled together.

"Why the long faces?" Caelum asked with a Cheshire grin.

They both glared up at him from behind their drinks. Caelum was the last to arrive. He sat down at the table, still grinning.

"What did you find?" Ariel asked, uninterested.

"Not just what, but who," Caelum replied.

"Out with it, demon," growled Charlotte impatiently.

"First, I would like to order a drink. I'm absolutely parched."

"Tell us what you know, or I'll gut you," she hissed.

"I'm on her side," Ariel chimed in.

"You two are so impatient," pouted Caelum. "Fine, I'll get on with it. The man you're looking for is Kingston Hale. He owns the Silver Stake, a brothel for the wealthy."

"And where are you goin', missy?" Ariel grumbled when Charlotte got up.

"I know where that is. I'm going to go kill him," she growled.

"Oh, no you're not," Caelum started. "He's wealthy and too well connected to just go after him like you are."

"I don't care who he is," she said, baring her fangs. "He dies tonight!"

Caelum looked over at Ariel, who sighed irritably before getting up.

"Let go of me," she screamed, kicking her legs when he lifted her off the ground.

Caelum followed Ariel as Charlotte was once again carried kicking and screaming obscenities out of another establishment.

"Ariel, let me go!" she cried.

"Not until you've calmed down," he replied, holding her tighter.

"He took my heart. Now I want his," she countered.

"And per our agreement, you'll have it," said Caelum. "But we have to be smart about it."

She looked Caelum dead in the eyes and said, "If you're too scared, then I'll go alone, but I don't care how powerful he is. He dies."

"And so will you," Caelum said softly after a moment.

"I. Don't. Care!"

Ariel roared in pain when she wretched her arms free and clawed his. He dropped her, and she sprinted away before he could grab her again.

"Damn, she's fast," he grunted, assessing his wounds. They were deep, but already healing. "Should we go after her?"

"No, let her go. You were right, she's far too wild," Caelum said solemnly. "Let's just go home. We'll start looking for Dolls again tomorrow."

Caelum had heard terrible things about Kingston Hale. He came from a long line of powerful, well-respected witches. In his lust for more power, he had betrayed his own kind and lost his family's legacy. He was dangerous and not without some skill.

With his head down, Caelum turned and started the journey home. Charlotte would have been a lovely Doll, and a better friend, but her grief and desire for revenge were too great for her to be of any use to them. So, with a heavy heart, he let his new friend go. He just hoped Charlotte survived.

CHAPTER 8

Over the next few days, Caelum and Ariel still had little luck in getting others interested in helping them build their Doll House. They got some interest from a few vampires and some dhampirs, and some cambions, but others were still too afraid to cross Kingston Hale by helping any competition. Caelum had discovered that not only was Hale a powerful witch, but he was blackmailing public officials. He was also kidnapping and trafficking supernatural beings, killing some for their parts to sell on the black market, while others were forced into servitude with the use of binding collars. All while he was presenting as an upstanding citizen, at least among the humans and wealthy. It made Caelum even more worried for Charlotte.

It did not take long before they realized that starting their business while Hale was in power would be potentially dangerous. His permission would be needed, but there was no guarantee he would give his blessing. Hale's supporters warned them to stop asking for help, especially since they would compete directly with Hale. Other brothels had to answer to him and give him a cut of their profits. Caelum did not want that, and he was not about to give up either.

"I think we should call it a night, Cae. It's getting late and Hale might be out with his people," said Ariel in a tired voice.

Caelum yawned and stretched. "Perhaps you're right. We've made some progress over the last few days, and I'm getting hungry."

"For food or people?" he grinned.

"You already know the answer to that, but I'll make you something before I feed," Caelum replied as he walked away.

Shortly after they got home, they heard a knock at their door, though it sounded more like a thud from something falling onto it. When they opened it, Ariel had barely caught her when she fell. Charlotte appeared beaten and bruised, with her tail wrapped around her leg. She looked to be on the verge of tears before she passed out. Ariel lifted her in his arms and carried her to their bed.

Caelum tended to her wounds the way Roland had taught him. Ever since he left, he had made a habit of keeping medicinal herbs in his home in case of emergencies. After a few hours, Charlotte woke up.

"What on earth happened to you?" Caelum asked. "Don't move too much. You have broken ribs, and you're healing slowly."

He helped her sit up and gave her a cup of water.

"I found Hale," she replied, choking on the water. "Where's Ariel?"

"He's out patrolling the perimeter in case you were followed. Hale did this to you?"

She nodded, wincing as she did so. "He tried to break me so he could add me to one of his brothels, but I got free and came here."

"How did you find us?"

"I just asked where the two pretty men who were asking about dolls lived," she yawned, laying back down.

Before he could ask her more questions, she had already fallen back to sleep.

"How is she?" came Ariel in the doorway.

Caelum turned to face him. "A bit worse for wear, but she'll be fine with a little more rest." He got up and walked past Ariel, closing the door behind him. "Apparently, Hale did that to her."

"I believe it," said Ariel, folding his arms over his broad chest. "For a human, he's a monster."

"Was she followed here?"

"So far, no. Things are getting dangerous, Caelum. Maybe we should stop poking the hornet's nest?"

"I'm not giving up, Ariel. We'll find a way around Hale."

"I wish I shared your optimism," he grumbled. "But I'm with you, no matter how this turns out."

"Good. I didn't think you were the type to run from a fight," Caelum said with a smirk.

Caelum continued to tend to Charlotte while Ariel kept watch over the property. After half a week, Charlotte was better and moving around again. Caelum realized she had been given something that slowed her healing ability. Once it was out of her system, she healed up quickly. It made him wonder what kind of dark magic Hale was into that could incapacitate a Nevala's healing.

Once Charlotte was better and things seemed to calm again, the three of them went in search of alliances against Hale. They started with the vampires since they had not fallen prey to Hale's blackmail, but have been hunted by him. The three of them requested an audience with the vampire queen to plead their case, but the queen only allowed Caelum to see her.

They took Caelum to what he assumed was supposed to be the throne room. The vampires of London lived in a large mansion in the wealthy part of the city. The halls were dimly lit, adorned with tapestries depicting the long history of Ximena's reign. When the silent, pale-faced guards dropped him off, Ximena sat in a large, plush chair, her presence commanding and otherworldly.

"Why does an incubus dare to enter my domain?" Ximena's voice was like silk, smooth, yet it carried an edge of danger.

Caelum bowed deeply. "Your Majesty, I come seeking an alliance. Kingston Hale has grown bolder and has become increasingly dangerous to your kind and others like us."

Ximena's eyes narrowed, her gaze piercing through Caelum. "And why should I trust a lowly sex demon? Your kind are near extinction. What do you offer that could possibly be of interest to me?"

Caelum took a deep breath, his mind racing. "I offer my loyalty and a safe feeding ground for those of you willing to work with me."

Ximena leaned back as she considered his words. The room was silent, the tension palpable. Finally, she spoke, "Very well, demon. I will form this alliance, but know this: betray me, and you will wish for death."

Caelum nodded, a wave of relief washing over him. "I understand, your Majesty."

"Oh, and a couple of other things: you must see to it that Hale leaves my people alone. He doesn't allow us in his brothels, and feeding on willing donors is harder because of him."

Caelum furrowed his brow. "I don't understand what you want of me, my Lady."

"We need to find the source of his power and destroy it. Kill him if you must. He needs to be stopped for the sake of all creatures," she explained.

Caelum swallowed hard. "But, my Lady–"

"I insist on it. That is, if you want this alliance," she purred.

He sighed in defeat. "Very well, your Majesty."

"Ximena," she corrected.

"Ximena. Was there anything else?"

"Yes," she grinned behind fangs. "A blood pact. We will seal our deal in blood."

He could see the luster of need in her eyes. "Of course, I understand."

Ximena was strikingly beautiful. She had stunning violet eyes that seemed to pierce through the darkness. Her hair was a cascade of pure white, contrasting beautifully with her rich brown skin. She exuded an aura of timeless elegance and power, her presence both captivating and intimidating. Her eyes held centuries of wisdom and secrets, while her hair flowed like a silken river, only adding to her ethereal and otherworldly beauty. And she wanted him.

She led Caelum through a door to the side of her throne, to a bedchamber. In the center of the room was a large, four-poster canopy bed. She disrobed and plopped down on the bed, beckoning him to her as she licked her full lips. Caelum was nervous at first, but remembered he could not feed on the dead. Ximena was safe from his demonic need, but he was not safe from hers.

"Remove your clothes," she commanded.

He was reluctant, but did as ordered. He tried to keep in mind that she would not kill him. She needed him. They had a common enemy.

His erection stood tall with a need of its own. She smiled broadly, pleased with what she saw. She raised one of her long, shapely legs in his direction, a silent order for him to come closer and touch her. He obliged her, taking hold of her bare foot, her ankle adorned with a gold bangle. He blazed a trail of kisses up the inside of her calf and thigh. Kneeling down on the ground, his face perfectly aligned between her thighs.

With excruciating slowness, Caelum continued to kiss and dote on the supple skin of her inner thighs, his teeth grazing the sensitive flesh. Each brush of his lips made her squirm and whimper, her hands in tight fists in his dirty blond hair.

"I will make my Lady scream with pleasure," he murmured, his breath searing the flesh of her sensitive core.

And then his mouth was on her. She gasped at the sensations of his warm, wet tongue delving between her folds. She threw her head back, and she cried out as he sucked the most delicate part of her with unyielding focus, his hands keeping her spread wide for his work. Ximena continued to whimper as her hips rocked against his face. He groaned against her, sending the vibrations rattling through her. His tongue swirled around her clit before he sucked it into his mouth, making her scream when he lightly bit down on it.

"Mm, yes, my pet," she panted, her fingers tightening in his hair. "Right there."

She held him in place, making him smile. He continued to lick and suck with such intensity that he had her shaking around him. He could feel she was getting close to coming when he felt her walls tighten around his tongue. Then, with an almost hoarse cry, her hips arched off the bed as she came undone on his tongue. He held her as wave after wave of pleasure crashed over her.

When she came down from her high, she fell back on the bed, her breathing labored and her body limp. Caelum remained where he was, lapping her up through the quakes of her desire. He pulled back once he was satisfied, and gazed up at her. His blue-green eyes lit with his own need as he licked his lips of her arousal.

"My Lady tastes exquisite," he said, brushing his lips over the skin of her inner thigh again. "I could gorge myself upon your flesh all night."

She sighed, her body trembling from the feel of his words on her skin and her release. Caelum got to his feet, taking a moment to admire the rise and fall of her ample breasts as she stared up at him. The fire of her desire had not yet gone out. She wanted more of him, and he was all too happy to give it to her. He captured her lips in a fierce kiss, allowing her to taste herself on his mouth. His hands moved over her curves almost possessively, getting another moan out of her. She arched into his touch, begging for more contact.

"Ximena," he purred, his voice deep with need.

His mouth found her throat, then he nipped and licked a searing path to her to her breasts. He lowered his head, taking one erect nipple into his warm, wet mouth. His tongue swirled around the perky nub. She gasped and cried out when his teeth grazed it before sucking hard on it.

He chuckled. "Such lovely sounds, and so needy," he said against her breast.

She wriggled impatiently beneath him, desperately seeking more of the exquisite torture. "Please," she begged.

Again, he chuckled. "What does my Lady need?"

She merely growled in response.

"As you wish, your Majesty," he growled back.

He ran his nimble fingers between her slick slit, making her hiss, before he positioned the head of his cock at her throbbing entrance. He captured her lips in another heated kiss, then slid inside her without resistance. She broke their kiss as another gasp escaped her. He did not move. He wanted to give her time to adjust to his size. Despite his earlier work, she was still tight. It surprised him when she expertly rolled her hips, making him moan as he sunk deeper into her.

"Ah," she said in a breathy tone. "I need you to move now."

He nodded, then kissed her again as he slowly moved. He pulled out just enough, leaving only the head of his cock inside of her, then he sunk back into her, making her cry out again. She languished as his thick shaft dragged along her pulsating walls.

"Yes," she moaned when he set a steady, purposeful rhythm. "Just like that, my pet."

Her nails dug into his back as he pulled almost all the way out before driving back into her, all the way to the base of his cock. He groaned his approval when she wrapped her legs around his waist, arching her hips to take more of him in. At that angle, his control slipped. His speed increased, moving faster and hitting harder. With each thrust, they grew closer to release. His breathing became ragged as his thrusts were more erratic. He could feel her inner walls lock around him as he sought his own release. She howled out, bucking wildly beneath him, triggering his climax. His cock pulsed and throbbed inside her, spilling his hot seed into her welcoming body.

He sucked in a sharp breath when he felt the prick of her fangs in his throat. She clung to him in a vice-like grip as she drank her fill of him. And once she was done, she collapsed, releasing him. He thought of pulling out and leaving, but he knew that would only offend her. So, he brought her delicate wrist to his mouth and bit down, drawing her blood into him. When he had enough, he pulled out of her and passed out next to her. The blood pact was complete.

CHAPTER 9

So, how did things go?" Ariel grinned knowingly.

Caelum appeared hours later, smelling of sex. His shirt had blood on the collar and the back. He would need to feed soon to heal the wounds completely.

"We have the alliance," Caelum grumbled, blushing as he walked past Ariel and Charlotte.

"I should hope so," spat Charlotte bitterly. "We were out here for hours."

"Yes, sorry about that," said Caelum, continuing to walk as far away from the mansion as he could get.

Ximena had an insatiable appetite and woke up wanting to fuck again... several times. Caelum was grateful he could even keep up, but he was exhausted now.

"Well, what did she say?" she asked impatiently, confused by his behavior.

Ariel only continued to grin as he followed the two of them.

"She ordered us to kill Hale," he muttered.

"We were already planning to do that. Is she going to help?"

"No, not with that. We have to prove ourselves first."

"Hold on a minute," she said, grabbing him by the shoulder and stopping him. "What's the point of an alliance if she's not going to even help?"

"It's all right, Lottie. We can do this on our own," he tried, but he was not as sure as he sounded.

"The hell we can! He's got power, and he has a large pack under him for protection." She was fuming, but there was no fear behind her anger. "I barely escaped with my life."

"I know, but we can do this if we stick together. We won't have to worry about that pack when the time comes," he explained. "That's one thing she was willing to help with."

"How are we supposed to get him?" Ariel asked, finally breaking his silence.

"That's the simple part. He's throwing a party tomorrow evening that we are to attend," Caelum replied.

"Are you mad?" asked Charlotte, bewildered.

"Charlotte, please. We can do this. I promised you his heart, and I intend to keep that promise."

"Ariel, say something!"

"Oh, no. Once he's got somethin' in his head, there's no talkin' him out of it," Ariel replied flatly.

She threw up her arms in exasperation. "Fine, he'll make slaves of us all."

The three of them continued their journey back to Caelum's home. They needed to make a plan before attending Hale's party. His dream of a better life was on the line, and Caelum refused to give up on it. Especially now that he had Ariel and Charlotte to worry about. They needed a place to belong, just as he did. He would not let the likes of Kingston Hale get in the way of what he wanted.

The brothel, known as the Silver Stake, sat atop a large hill in London. It was the night of the blood moon, and the mansion came alive with a lavish party, drawing in wealthy supernaturals and humans from all over. Hale held this kind of party whenever there was a celestial occurrence that did not happen often. Rumors circulated about rituals performed at the parties that kept the wealthy in power. It all needed to stop.

The grand hall boasted chandeliers made of the finest crystals, their flames flickering with an eerie blue light. Draped in velvet, the walls shimmered with enchantments that whispered secrets to those who dared to listen. A haunting melody played by invisible musicians filled the air, setting the perfect tone for the evening.

Among the guests were werewolves and shapeshifters who shifted forms seamlessly, their eyes glowing with the thrill of the night. There were also dark fairies in attendance, their allure undeniable as they mingled with the humans.

Some humans were snorting a dark substance that glittered slightly. Others were licking it off various parts of prostitutes, and a few were ingesting it via wine. There was even one person inserting a glass plug into a woman's rectum that was covered with the stuff. Caelum recognized it as vampire ashes mixed with fairy bones. It was an illegal substance that was obtained without mercy. They kept the fairies alive as long as possible and took their bones bit by bit. The vampires did not fare as well; they were burned alive and their ashes collected.

They called the illicit drug Elysia because of the heavenly high one got from taking it. It had a blood-red hue that shimmered with the dust of the crushed fairy bones. The powder was often laced with an aphrodisiac to help those with weak libidos. Once the powder was in their system, their eyes glowed a vibrant red. They suddenly became sexually aggressive and went after the person closest to them. Limited magical abilities and enhanced strength were also side effects of the drug.

The high from it was almost immediate, but it wore off after an hour, sometimes less, depending on the age of the source. Hunters created the drug as a means of gathering information. Elysia was addictive and made it easy to blackmail people who enjoyed the substance. There have been those that have overdosed on it. Their bodies would eventually burn out and wither away.

At the center of the room stood a table laden with dark magical items. Amulets and crystal orbs, as well as a dagger forged in the fires of the underworld, lay on the table, its blade humming with a thirst for blood. There was also a large supply of Elysia for anyone to partake in.

Caelum had made it a point to keep Charlotte close to stop any unwanted female attention. Though there was the random brush of his arm whenever they passed someone, followed by a suggestive smile. Ariel stayed behind them to keep any others away, but even he was getting unwanted attention. The three of them did their best to blend in and not draw attention to themselves as they stepped over the occasional engaged couple.

As the night progressed, Hale had yet to show himself. Soon, the room erupted in the sounds of mating. They noticed many supernatural creatures being used as unwilling sex slaves with control collars on, several black market items in use, and human public officials taking part in orgies while ingesting Elysia. There was not a single vampire or even a dhampir among the slaves or piles of naked flesh. He wondered what Hale had against them that he did not include them.

It was all just a sensory overload.

"Caelum, are you all right?" asked Charlotte. She noticed that Caelum's breathing had become labored, and he was sweating profusely.

"Shit," Ariel said through gritted teeth. "We need to leave. Now."

"What's wrong?" she asked, her brow furrowed.

"This was a bad idea," Ariel growled, taking hold of Caelum.

"Wait, is he an incubus?"

"Yes, and keep your voice down," he hissed as he took Caelum out of the mansion with Charlotte on his heels. "We need to get him some place safe to feed."

"My place isn't too far from here. We can go there," she offered.

Ariel threw a catatonic Caelum over his shoulder as he and Charlotte hurried to her home.

Once they arrived, Ariel demanded to know where the bedroom was.

"Upstairs. Last door on the right," she replied, unsure of what was happening.

Ariel ascended the stairs two at a time. Then he was in the room. He kicked the door closed and threw Caelum onto the bed. Quickly, he stripped out of his suit and removed Caelum's. Caelum was still unresponsive, his face a mask of nothing. Ariel grabbed his face and laid a fierce kiss on his lips. Still,

Caelum did not respond, but he could tell he was fighting his transformation.

Ariel dropped to his knees. He knew what happened when Caelum got like that. He would transform, then become intangible and float off to some unsuspecting person's home if he could not get at someone nearby. Caelum would kill again, and Ariel did not want that for him. He wrapped his mouth around the head of Caelum's cock, his tongue swirling around the rim with expert care and control. At that, Caelum responded. Ariel saw the mask of nothing turn into one of lust.

With a sigh of relief, Ariel continued his work, but Caelum stopped him. Caelum took hold of Ariel's face and kissed him slowly, his tongue sweeping across Ariel's, entreating entrance. Ariel opened and welcomed Caelum in. The kiss started with tenderness, whispering of what was to come, but the heat built up. Their hunger was growing. Caelum stood, bringing Ariel with him and not breaking their kiss. His hands found Ariel's rear, kneading the firm muscles, pulling the wolf against him. Ariel moaned at the contact. Caelum spun Ariel around, laying him down on the bed.

With his body on top of Ariel's, Caelum positioned himself at his entrance. The head of his prick pushed past stubborn muscles, getting a grunt from Ariel, then he sunk his shaft in, inch by glorious inch. Ariel took hold of Caelum's ass and forced him in deeper. This time, Caelum grunted. Ariel was always so tight at first. He started a steady rhythm after taking a moment to adjust to Ariel's hole.

Ariel rolled his hips as Caelum thrusted into him. They kissed as they fucked. There was no emotion other than carnal need as Ariel's life force flowed into Caelum. He pumped into Ariel until Ariel's cock erupted, his seed spilling on his stomach and chest. When Caelum heard a gasp at the door, he turned quickly to see Charlotte standing there with her fingers buried deep in her own hole.

In an instant, Caelum was in front of her. He pressed her into the wall, locking her stunned gaze with his as he removed her hand and replaced it with his own. A gasp turned into a moan when he found her. He brought his hand up to his lips and licked her sweetness off his fingers, not once breaking eye contact. She could taste her arousal on his lips when he kissed her. As his tongue swept over her lips, he grabbed ahold of her thighs and lifted her above his waist. He notched the head of his cock at her entrance, then, when he deepened their kiss, he drove his cock inside her. There was no resistance. She was so wet from watching him with Ariel and pleasuring herself.

Charlotte rocked her hips eagerly, meeting each of his thrusts. She dug her claws into his shoulders as he pumped her furiously against the wall. He ran his tongue across her throat, nipping lightly at her collarbone. Her energy slowly flowed into him just as Ariel's had. He pounded her harder the closer he got to climax. She threw her head back as she came undone around him.

Once he had his fill of her essence, he released his seed into her, riding out her waves of ecstasy with her. When she finally came down from the high of her release, he carried her to the bed and laid her beside a sleeping Ariel. Shortly after, he collapsed into unconsciousness with them.

CHAPTER 10

C aelum woke up, greeted by the dim light filtering through heavy curtains. The room was shrouded in shadows, with only a few slivers of dawn breaking through. He sat up slowly, his head buzzing and his vision slightly blurred. The bed beneath him was unfamiliar—luxurious, with dark, silken sheets that felt cool against his skin.

He glanced around the room, noticing it was filled with antique furniture. There was a grand wardrobe with intricate designs carved into it, a vanity with an ornate mirror, and a fireplace. The air was thick with the scent of old wood and a hint of something floral, perhaps lavender.

His heart raced as he tried to piece together the events of the previous night, but his mind was blank. He swung his legs over the side of the bed, feeling the plush carpet beneath his feet. A sense of unease settled in his stomach as he stood, his legs shaky. Putting on a pair of pants lying on the floor, he moved toward the window. He pulled back the curtains and was met with a view of a misty forest; the trees standing like silent sentinels. The scene was both beautiful and eerie.

"Malcom loved that view," came a soft, sad voice.

Caelum turned to see Charlotte leaning against the wall by the door. She wore a shirt that was three sizes too big for her. It hung off one shoulder and showed off her long, shapely legs. She hugged herself with the memory of her mate, her fingers rubbing a scale pendant.

"It's a lovely view," he said with a soft smile. "Where's Ariel?"

"He's out running, though I don't know where he got the energy," she yawned.

"I see," he responded, avoiding eye contact. The events of the previous evening suddenly returned to him.

"You should have told me you were an incubus," she said, her tone holding a slight edge to it.

"My apologies. I just–"

"Spare me your excuses," she yawned again, waving him off. "We all have secrets, though yours is dangerous."

"Yes, and I'd appreciate it if it stayed a secret."

"You have my word," she said, giving a slight nod. She pushed off the wall and joined him at the window. "Where's your coven?"

He let out a sigh, turning to stare at the trees. "I don't have one. Haven't had one since I was a boy." He turned to look at her. "You and Ariel are all I have. Well, you and the people that found and raised me."

"Where are they now?"

"In Wales."

They continued to chat, getting to know one another better. Caelum had relayed how he was found and why he was banished from his coven. He told her how he found Ariel and how they became friends. She told him about her life with Malcom, her mate, before he died. He was a good bit older than her, but that did not matter to her. Since there were no Andr left, they worked as bounty hunters. It was not a life she enjoyed, but she loved her mate and would do anything for him. It broke her when he died in her arms. The Andr pendant was all that she had left of him now.

After an hour had passed, Ariel had returned, but he was not alone. He had brought a vampire with him. She seemed shy and badly shaken, as if she had a rough night as well. It was an odd thing to see a vampire out during the day. However, she was wearing clothes that covered her body from head to toe. Had she not uncovered her face, they would have thought she was something else.

"Tell them what you told me," Ariel ordered.

The girl winced at the gruff sound of his command. "Her Majesty has sent me with a message about Kingston Hale."

Caelum and Charlotte sat at the large wooden table in the dining room. They were not expecting to hear from Queen Ximena so soon.

"Well, out with it," growled Charlotte impatiently.

Again, the vampire winced. "Queen Ximena says that the source of Hale's power is a demon pact."

"How does she know this?" asked Caelum.

"The queen has many spies," the vampire explained. "It's late, I must go to ground soon. Her Majesty orders you to find the object that binds him to the demon and banish it."

"How in the bloody hell are we supposed to do that?" asked Charlotte.

The vampire shrugged, then put her cover back on her head. She bowed at the waist before she turned to leave.

"I don't understand. If her Majesty has spies in Hale's house, why not have one of them kill him?" asked Ariel.

"Hunters that use dark magic aren't easy to get to like that. They're paranoid and trust no one, and they're light sleepers," Caelum explained. "One with a demon pact would be more than difficult to get the drop on."

"Then what do we do?" asked Charlotte.

"We get the name of the demon and banish them," Caelum answered.

"Any ideas on how we do that?" Ariel questioned.

"No," Caelum sighed, burying his face in his hands as they rested on the table.

Ariel placed a reassuring hand on Caelum's shoulder. "You'll figure it out," he started. "We'll get rid of Hale, and you'll get your Doll House."

"I'm glad one of us believes that," Caelum smiled wryly, looking up at him.

The three of them nearly jumped out of their skin when they heard a loud thunk in the front door. When they went to investigate, there was a thick, heavy, blood-stained stake splintering the wood of the door. Ariel took the lead and opened the door slowly. On the other side was the body of the vampire messenger, her body mangled and broken in a bloody and grizzly display as it hung. Caelum squeezed past Ariel, who was scanning the area protectively, to remove the blood-stained letter pinned to the poor girl.

As he read the note, his blood boiled. "Get her down," he growled out, crumpling the letter in a tight fist. "Threaten us all you want! We will not be stopped," he shouted at no one.

"What the hell, Cae?" growled Ariel as he pulled the long wooden stake out of the door.

"Hale knows who we are now," he responded through gritted teeth.

Charlotte took the letter from him and read it aloud. "Give up or die, incubus scum."

"Fuck," said Ariel. He pulled the dead vampire from off the stake and laid her down, tossing the stake off to the side.

"Caelum, he knows what you are," said Charlotte.

"It doesn't matter," he replied. "I won't give up."

"But he'll kill you," she pleaded.

"He can try."

"I was hoping you'd say that," came an unfamiliar, deep, rumbling voice.

Ariel growled low in his chest, his muscles tensed.

"Ariel! How long has it been?" said the mystery figure coming from the side of the house.

"Draven," Ariel snarled.

The three of them stepped outside as Draven came into full view. To say that he was imposing would be a great disservice to how massive he truly was. He dwarfed Ariel, which Caelum did not believe was possible.

"How's the rogue life treating you?" Two others flanked Draven, but they were so much smaller they might as well not have been there. "I see you're bedding down with an incubus—and a Nevala?" He winked at Charlotte. "My, how you've fallen."

"You know that giant asshole?" spat Charlotte, recoiling.

"Yes, he's the leader of a rival pack in London." Ariel kept his eyes locked on Draven as he spoke, and a protective stance in front of Caelum and Charlotte.

"We're no longer rivals, Ariel. You don't have a pack," said Draven. "In fact, your old pack is now blended with mine. The old and new leaders are dead," he grinned wickedly.

Caelum could see the hackles on Ariel's neck stand on end in rage.

"I'll kill you," Ariel growled low.

Caelum and Charlotte watched as Ariel's skin split to reveal the charcoal gray fur underneath. Bones broke and knitted back together as he shifted from a standing position to all fours.

"Do you really want to do this?" laughed Draven.

Ariel snapped his lupin jaws at Draven in response.

"All right, then."

Caelum and Charlotte moved back into the house when Draven shifted. He was a massive beast with dark, shaggy fur, and eyes that burned like embers. He let out a low growl that echoed through the trees. His muscles rippled under his fur, and his claws dug into the earth, ready to strike. Ariel was only slightly smaller and no less intimidating, his piercing blue eyes filled with a cold determination.

The surrounding silence was shattered as Draven lunged forward, his claws slashing through the air. Ariel, being smaller, dodged with lightning speed, countering with a powerful swipe that left deep gashes in his opponent's side. Blood sprayed across the ground, but Draven barely flinched, driven by sheer rage and dominance.

They circled each other, snarling and snapping, each looking for an opening. Draven charged again, this time feinting to the left before striking from the right. Ariel anticipated the move and caught Draven's arm in his powerful jaws and shook it violently. Draven roared in pain but managed to wrench free, delivering a brutal kick that sent Ariel sprawling.

For a moment, Ariel laid still, the wind knocked out of him. But he regained his footing, his eyes blazing with renewed fury. He launched himself at Draven, their bodies colliding with a force that shook the ground. They tumbled and rolled, a blur of fur and fangs, each trying to gain the upper hand.

Each alpha pushed their limits. Those around them held their breath, the only sounds the growls and snarls of the combatants and the occasional snap of a branch under their weight.

Finally, with great effort, Ariel managed to pin Draven to the ground, his jaws closing around his opponent's throat. Draven struggled, but Ariel's grip was unyielding. With a final, desperate snarl, Draven went limp, a wet snap and crunch echoing through the trees.

Ariel released his grip, his mouth covered in so much blood as he stood tall and proud over his fallen rival. The forest seemed to exhale; the tension dissipating as quickly as it had come. Ariel let out a mournful but triumphant howl, his victory echoing through the air, a testament to his strength and dominance.

He snapped at the two other wolves Draven had brought with him. The pair quickly collected the body of their fallen alpha and left once Ariel stepped away. Though he moved away, he kept watch over the two of them in case they tried anything. Once they were out of sight, Ariel shifted back to his human form and collapsed.

Caelum and Charlotte rushed to his side and quickly got him back inside. They noticed the bruise forming on his left side where he had been kicked. Caelum was sure his ribs were broken. They got him into bed, and Caelum bandaged him up as best he could with the bedding he ripped. Charlotte protested the destruction of her sheets, but helped him anyway.

"Will he be all right?" she asked.

"With some rest, yes," Caelum replied. "He shouldn't have fought with such little energy. I know I took a lot from him last night."

"He seemed so sad at the end."

"That's to be expected. That monster wolf killed the leader of his pack."

Charlotte wrinkled her nose in confusion. "Why was he sad about that? They banished him."

"The old leader banished him. His son was the new leader and Ariel's former lover, that he was forced to leave behind," he explained.

Her eyes went wide. "Oh."

Caelum sat down next to Ariel and watched him sleep. They were no longer safe. Kingston would only send more after them. He could not give up now.

CHAPTER 11

They had slept in shifts to watch over Ariel. Caelum had taken the first watch so Charlotte could regain the strength he had taken from her. She had nudged him awake the next morning due to all the commotion going on outside. Several dozen werewolves had gathered outside of her home and set up multiple camps on the property. Some were trying to peek through the windows.

"Why are there wolves piling up outside?" Caelum asked, blurry eyed.

"How am I supposed to know? I'm not a wolf," she replied.

It suddenly dawned on him what they wanted. "Ariel will not be happy when he wakes up."

"I'm not happy about this either! One wolf in my house is enough."

"They must be from Draven's pack. They most likely believe Ariel to be their new alpha."

"What's with all the noise?" Ariel grumbled, coming down the stairs.

"You really shouldn't be up," Caelum fussed.

Ariel growled and snapped his jaws in response. Caelum narrowed his eyes, but said nothing more. Ariel stepped outside wearing only a pair of pants he found in the wardrobe and his bedsheet bandages, shielding his eyes from the light of the morning sun.

Several wolves looked up at Ariel and smiled. Mothers urged their pups forward to greet their new alpha. They were scared at first, but their curiosity won out over their fear. Ariel regarded the pups that ran over to him with a stern face but gentle eyes. The pups giggled as they took turns showing their respect to their alpha before running back to their mothers.

Caelum and Charlotte stood dumbfounded as adults did the same, and Ariel accepted it. Werewolves were complicated creatures. Caelum fully expected Ariel to reject them all. Ariel would have a proper family now. He would not need him anymore. It would just be him and Charlotte now if she did not want to leave him. The thought of losing Ariel made him sad, but he knew it was for the best.

Sensing his melancholy, Charlotte bumped his shoulder with hers and smiled at him. He returned her smile, then gave her a light squeeze.

Ariel turned and saw the exchange. "What did I miss?" he asked, walking back over to them.

"Nothing," said Caelum. "We're just happy for you."

"You don't look all that happy," Ariel countered. "You don't think I'm abandoning you after all this?"

"Well, you're a pack leader now. You have others to care for," Caelum replied.

"Yes, and that still includes you. I'm not going to let Hale kill you—either of you," he said, looking at both of them. "My pack is your pack."

"That's all well and good, Ariel, but where are they going to stay?" asked Charlotte as her tail twitched from side to side in irritation.

Ariel chuckled. "Don't worry, they have their own homes on land just outside of the city. They only came here to greet me."

"Well, they've seen you. Make them leave, please."

"They will once I've chased those still loyal to Draven out. His beta has taken over, and they're still working for Hale," Ariel explained. "So, please be patient with them."

A young wolf timidly walked up to them, his hands clasped together and his shoulders hunched as if he were trying to make himself small. He could not have been more than sixteen or seventeen. He was thin, underfed.

"Um, alpha?" he squeaked.

"Yes, what is it?" Ariel answered sternly.

"I have some information that might be helpful to you," he replied.

"Out with it, boy," Ariel growled impatiently.

Again, the boy squeaked and flinched at Ariel's tone. "Um, it's about Kingston Hale."

The mention of Hale's name got Caelum's attention. "What do you know?"

The boy looked at Caelum, then back to Ariel, who nodded his permission. "He talks to a demon named Dagon. He has an amulet that he almost never takes off that controls the demon."

"How do you know all this?" asked Caelum.

"I overheard Draven and the others talking about it," the boy answered.

"Is that all?" Ariel inquired.

The boy nodded. "Yes, alpha."

Ariel looked at Caelum, who looked white as a ghost. He dismissed the boy and turned his full attention to Caelum. "Are you all right?"

"Dagon is an upper-level demon lord," Caelum answered, a hint of fear in his voice.

"What does that matter? We only need to banish him. That should be easy enough."

Caelum's eyes went wide. "No, it's not," he started. "Hale's life belongs to that demon. Hale controls nothing where Dagon is concerned."

"You certainly know a lot about him," Charlotte mentioned.

"Of course I do. He's my father," Caelum admitted.

Ariel and Charlotte paled at that.

"Well, shit," said Ariel after a few moments. "What do you want to do now?"

Caelum set his jaw. They were fucked if Dagon was involved. But they would be killed if they did nothing about him. They had to go forward. Kingston Hale needed to be stopped.

"Caelum?" Charlotte called worriedly when he stood there staring off at nothing.

"We fight," he said after another moment. "We summon my father and get him to leave willingly."

"And if that doesn't work?" Ariel asked.

"We get the amulet and banish him. The amulet tethers him to this plane. Without it, he can't stay here."

"Then let's get to work banishing a demon," said Ariel.

After careful research, Caelum had found the proper summoning ritual for an upper-level demon. Dagon was a powerful demon lord, feared and revered by many. It made Caelum wonder why his father would bind himself to Kingston Hale, of all people. Hale was a formidable witch, but he was human. What could he have had to offer a demon lord that was worth what he had?

His mother had talked about Dagon often, fawning over the demon as if he was a god. Even his sisters walked around proudly, but not Caelum. He did not understand the appeal. He felt like an outcast even before he got ill. Dagon had never been a part of their lives. It made him wonder how his mother met him in the first place. She never mentioned it, and most demons—lords included—had to be summoned.

Caelum sighed as he readied himself to face his father for the first time. He made use of his basement, not wanting to cause further damage to Charlotte's home, and carved out the ancient runes he needed into a circle. He stood at the edge of the circle, the ancient runes glowing at his feet, and with a deep breath, he began the incantation to summon his father.

Ariel grumbled in a corner as the air crackled with energy. A portal opened, and Dagon emerged, his presence overwhelming. Dagon's appearance was a terrifying blend of majesty and horror. He stood at an imposing height, his form cloaked in shadows that seemed to writhe and pulse with a life of their own. His skin was a deep, obsidian black, and covered in scales that shimmered with an iridescent sheen. They shifted from deep purples to fiery reds as he moved.

Dagon's hands ended in long, clawed fingers, each tipped in talons that could rend flesh and bone with ease. His face was strikingly handsome, angular and sharp, with high cheekbones and a strong jawline. Around his neck hung a chain of dark iron, from which dangled a pendant inscribed with ancient runes of power and domination.

When he spoke, his voice was a deep, resonant growl that echoed with the weight of timeless, forbidden knowledge. "Caelum," his voice rumbled like thunder. "Why have you summoned me here?"

Caelum's voice trembled, but he stood firm. Though it surprised him that Dagon knew his name. "Father, I seek to banish you from this plane."

Dagon's laughter echoed through the room. "You think you can banish me, boy? You are but a shadow of my power."

"That may be, but it's enough to do away with you," Caelum said firmly.

"Is it now?" he purred. "Didn't seem like enough to keep you alive."

Caelum glared hard at his father, only getting a wide smile in response.

"Tell me, how is your mother? She was as lovely as they come, and lovelier still when she came over, and over, and over again. She tasted so sweet. It's a shame she birthed such weak progeny."

"How should I know? She abandoned me because of that damned demon pox," Caelum replied bitterly.

Dagon's eyes glowed with a malevolent light at the implications.

"Enough of this talk, father. I need you to leave this plane," he demanded.

Dagon smiled broadly again. "Why should I? I'm having so much fun here."

"Your servant is dangerous and needs to be stopped," Caelum countered. "If you won't leave willingly, I'll make you."

Dagon's expression darkened. "You would dare betray your own blood?"

"I would choose my own path," Caelum replied. "My life and that of my friends mean more to me than you ever could."

"You'll die, boy," Dagon snarled.

"Wouldn't be the first time," Caelum said with a smirk.

"Your god won't save you a second time," he chuckled. "Your new life will not last."

"Then I'll enjoy what time I have."

With a roar of fury, Dagon lunged at Caelum, but the summoning circle flared to life and held him at bay. Caelum began the chant to close the circle and the portal it opened, his voice steady and resolute. The air grew thick with magic as the runes glowed brighter and Dagon's form wavered.

"You cannot escape your fate!" Dagon bellowed.

Caelum's resolve did not waver. As the last words of the incantation left his lips, a blinding light filled the room. The portal closed with a deafening crash, and Caelum collapsed to his knees, exhausted. He would need to feed again to regain his strength.

Every aspect of Dagon's appearance exuded an aura of dread and authority, a testament to his status as a demon lord of immense power and malevolence. Opening a portal strong enough to summon him took a lot out of Caelum. Ariel rushed to his side when he saw he was about to fall over. The last thing Caelum saw was Ariel's worried face. He wondered when his second life would end as he drifted off to sleep.

CHAPTER 12

Tensions were high when they went back to the Silver Stake. Ariel had picked his strongest wolves to fight with them, but there were not many, only a handful at best. Thankfully, Ximena sent some of her strongest fighters to aid them.

Trying to convince Dagon to leave willingly went as expected, but now they would have an angry demon lord to worry about. Hale would be ready for them.

The plan was for Caelum to go in alone. Both Ariel and Charlotte protested, but he insisted. This was his fight, and he needed them to keep Hale's forces at bay.

The brothel was clear of any guests, but what remained of Draven's loyalists stood guard. The vampires, Charlotte, Ariel, and his wolves engaged them while Caelum snuck through to get into the mansion. He cautiously worked his way through each hall until he reached the main dining area. There, Hale sat in a large chair at the head of a long table. He was having dinner.

"Caelum Evans," Hale said, wiping his mouth with a decorative cloth. "It's good to finally put a face to the name."

"Same," Caelum replied. "Though I can't say I'm impressed with what I see."

Hale raised his dark eyes to Caelum, a look of mild offense on his pale, slender face. "Same," he repeated. "How did you find out about me?"

"People talk. Why are you so hellbent on controlling supernaturals?"

"I have my reasons, boy. I will not explain them to you."

When Hale sat up fully, Caelum saw the glint of something metallic around his neck. It was a small, intricately crafted amulet, no larger than the palm of a hand. It was the twin of the one Dagon wore, and it radiated with the same aura of immense power and malevolence.

Hale smiled at Caelum's recognition. "A tool of subjugation I used on your father."

"You're a fool if you believe he's under your command."

"Then I guess I'm a fool. He's not happy with you, by the way."

"Fuck my father," Caelum spat. With a burst of speed, he lunged at Hale.

But Hale was ready. He raised his hand, and a burst of light and power sent Caelum sprawling in the opposite direction.

"Did you really think you could take me on?" he laughed, standing as Caelum staggered to his feet. "I command the power of a demon lord."

Caelum had the wind knocked out of him, but he would not be so easily defeated. His horns broke through his skin at his temples, curling around his ears like before. His fingers were tipped obsidian black as they extended into powerful talons. He looked up at a grinning Hale, his eyes blazing with determination.

"Come on then, show me your strength, boy," Hale taunted.

Caelum roared and charged at him. Hale clutched his gleaming amulet, that pulsed with an eerie, otherworldly light. His eyes glowed with arcane power. He raised his hand again and sent bolts of dark energy crackling through the air. The two forces collided in a burst of light and shadow. The impact shook the very foundations of the mansion and created gusts of wind that extinguished the torches, plunging the room into near darkness. Only the glow of the amulet and Caelum's eyes provided any illumination. Hale summoned a barrier of shimmering energy, but Caelum's claws tore through it with ease, leaving trails of sparks in their wake.

As the battle raged on, Kingston's spells grew more desperate, each more powerful than the last. He conjured tendrils of shadow to ensnare Caelum, but his strength was relentless. Caelum broke free of the tendrils and sent Hale sprawling to the ground.

Caelum loomed over the fallen witch, his eyes gleaming with triumph. "Your reign of terror ends tonight," he sneered, his foot planted firmly on Hale's chest as he reached for the amulet.

"I won't be defeated so easily!" Hale roared, gripping his amulet.

Another burst of light sent Caelum flying, hitting the ground hard when he landed a good distance from Hale. When he looked up, Hale was being covered with what looked like a living shadow until it enveloped him completely. The cloak of shadow pulsed like a heartbeat with a blood red light. Hale's eyes glowed the same demonic red as he bore a set of sharp teeth. The demonic Hale laughed malevolently as he stalked towards an unsteady Caelum. Hale's body was much larger and looked like Dagon. He had actually summoned the demon to possess his body.

"I should've killed you when you came to my party," said Hale, his voice an altered growl. "The nerve of you showing up uninvited." He grabbed Caelum by his collar. "I'll gladly rid the world of you and your ridiculous idea of a brothel." He slammed Caelum hard into the ground, cracking the stone. "Then I'll make slaves of your pets outside." He gripped

Caelum's hair in a tight fist and pulled him up to meet his gaze. "The female will be my personal toy. And she won't escape me a second time."

Caelum growled furiously at that and swung up as hard as he could, his hand in a tight fist, hitting Hale across the jaw.

Hale stumbled back, letting Caelum go. He spat out blood that burned like acid through the stone floor.

Caelum found his footing and went after Hale while he was off balance. He pounded his face with strength he did not know he had until Hale was on the ground. Breathing heavily, he snatched the amulet from Hale's neck and watched as the shadow cloak receded back into the amulet.

Hale screamed in fury as he struggled beneath Caelum's boot. Caelum stared at the amulet of his father. It was made of a rare obsidian-like stone with a smooth, almost glassy surface. Upon closer inspection, he saw faint, swirling patterns that resembled tendrils of smoke trapped in the stone. The patterns shifted and moved as if alive, giving the amulet an otherworldly, almost hypnotic quality.

The stone was encased in a delicate lattice of silver and gold, twisted together in an elaborate design that formed protective runes and sigils. At the center of the amulet, embedded within the obsidian stone, was a single, blood-red gem. The gem pulsed faintly behind the smokey tendrils, like a heartbeat.

Hale noticed Caelum's attraction to the stone and smiled. "It calls to you, doesn't it? The blood of your kin," he laughed. "It won't work for you, though."

Caelum looked down at Hale, his lip curled up into a defiant smirk. "It doesn't have to. I've no need of such things." He began the banishment ritual, chanting the ancient words that would sever Dagon's bond to their plane.

The amulet glowed with intense light.

"You can't do this!" Hale roared.

But Caelum's voice rose above the noise. The amulet shattered with the last words of the incantation, sending Dagon back into the void.

"No!" Hale cried.

Caelum merely grinned down at him, stepping away when Charlotte and Ariel arrived, bringing the light with them.

"You're not going to kill me?" Hale inquired, confused.

"I promised your heart to someone else," Caelum answered.

Charlotte stepped forward, passing her torch to Caelum. She picked Hale up by the collar of his shirt. "Why?" she growled. "Why did you kill my Malcom?"

Hale scoffed at her question.

"Answer me, damn it!" she roared, her fangs bared.

He winced and grunted when her claws pierced his flesh. Despite the pain, still he smiled. "Because Nevala venom is highly sought after on the black market. He made such wonderful noises when I extracted it from him. Though your venom is much more potent, but I took what I could get."

"You monster!" she growled through gritted teeth.

"I don't know how he escaped, but there was no way he could survive for long. Not after what I did to him. His pelt would have made a lovely rug," he laughed.

His own blood caught in his throat, silencing his laugh. She pulled her hand from his chest, and he went limp. She dropped his body, crushing his still-beating heart in her hand.

Caelum and Ariel kept their distance as she spat on Hale's corpse, then proceeded to tear it to shreds. Blood and tattered viscera went everywhere until she was out of flesh to claw apart. All that remained of Kingston Hale were blood-soaked bones.

Her enraged screams echoed through the halls. She dropped to her knees and buried her face in her bloodied hands as she cried. Ariel and Caelum wanted to comfort her, but feared any contact would cause her to lash out. So, they stood beside her in solidarity.

With Hale dead, Caelum knew there would be a power vacuum created in the supernatural underworld. It would be chaos for those vying for the power he held. So, he would have to fill that void until there was no need for it. He looked over to Ariel, who was watching Charlotte break Hale's bones to bash his skull in. Ariel had a look, and Caelum could not tell if he was horrified by what she was doing or amused by it. Either way, he was keeping his distance. Caelum smiled at his dysfunctional new family. He was happy he would not be alone any longer.

Once Charlotte had calmed down, the three of them headed back to her place, since it was closer. Caelum needed to feed and recharge his energies. Fighting Hale had taken a lot out of him. So much so that Ariel eventually had to carry him the rest of the way. The wolves in Ariel's pack that helped them fight saw themselves back to their territory, and the vampires went back to Ximena to give their report.

They had just gotten to Charlotte's home in time before Caelum regained enough strength to hop out of Ariel's arms and chase Charlotte up the stairs to her room. He had a lustful luster in his eyes, so much so that they glowed. Ariel knew what that meant— Caelum would be extra avaricious in his energy pull.

By the time Ariel arrived in the room, Caelum and Charlotte had already removed the rest of their clothes. Charlotte was still covered in blood, but that did not seem to matter to Caelum. He was smiling when she pushed him down onto the bed. She was not acting like a widow in mourning. She had avenged her mate and now she sought to reward the man that helped her do it.

Ariel watched as Caelum pulled her into his lap, forcing her to straddle him. She worked her hips in a circle, grinding against his erection before she raised up and eased him into her. She took a moment to adjust to him, his hands firmly on her hips, then she twisted her hips again. Her tail twitched and swished around as she rode him.

Not wanting to be left out, Ariel removed the tattered remains of his clothing and moved to join them. Charlotte pushed Caelum down, then reached up to kiss Ariel. Caelum took hold of Ariel's cock, stoking it lightly before encasing the head in his mouth.

While Caelum sucked Ariel off, Charlotte nibbled on his bottom lip. Caelum grabbed Charlotte's tail and pulled it gently. Charlotte gasped at the sensation, then growled at Caelum. She could see him smiling around Ariel's cock. When he did it again, she came almost instantly, crying out.

Ariel moved behind her, taking her by the thighs, and lifted her up, getting a surprised yelp from her. There was a wet pop when he dislodged her from Caelum. He gently eased her down on his still hard shaft, making her sigh. Caelum sat back up and watched as Ariel raised and lowered Charlotte slowly on him, making her moan as she wrapped her arms around his neck.

The view from where Caelum was sitting was beautiful. Her honey pot was dripping wet still and swollen with need as her breasts bounced ever so slightly with Ariel's movements. And the noises she made had his cock aching to be back inside her.

He stood, stroking himself, as he positioned the head of his prick at her pulsing entrance. He slipped back inside her with ease. As Ariel fucked her from behind, he pounded her in the front. She had a look of pure bliss on her face as they took her from both ends.

Caelum grabbed hold of her legs, and Ariel held her breasts. She felt so full with both of them inside her, then she felt Caelum's warm, wet mouth on one of her breasts and she moaned with delight.

Ariel and Caelum grunted and groaned as they had their way with Charlotte. Caelum could feel himself getting close, and he could feel their combined life force flowing into him through Charlotte. They both tasted wild, spicy, and sweet, but each of their flavors was unique. Charlotte was spicy, with a hint of citrus, while Ariel had a nutty, but sweet taste.

Their pace quickened as they all drew near to climax. Charlotte's walls fluttered as they closed in around them. The friction from their strokes driving her mad with ecstasy. She thought she would burst from all the pleasure. Ariel grunted his release, followed by Caelum, but still they pumped until Charlotte came screaming again.

Ariel and Caelum fell to their knees, their breathing labored, but they were careful not to hurt Charlotte. With what little strength he had left, Ariel pulled out of her and got back to his feet, carrying her to the bed. Caelum followed as they both laid down, curling around one another in a pile of naked, dirty flesh and limbs. It did not matter, though. They were content in their huddled mass as they fell asleep, surrounded by the love and strength of their bond.

CHAPTER 13

After some much needed rest, they celebrated their victory over Kingston Hale the following evening. Ariel's new pack had invited them to their grounds, where they had a grand feast prepared. The scent of pine filled the air, and they could hear the distant sound of a babbling brook. It was a stark contrast to the oppressive darkness that had once shrouded their lives.

Ariel stood in the center of the clearing, where a collection of homes surrounded. Around him, the werewolves howled in unison, their voices echoing through the trees, a triumphant chorus that spoke of their victory over the evil witch who had enslaved them for so long.

Hale did not use magic to bind them to him. He did not have to. Draven was under his command of his own free will, and Draven culled any who did not agree with what Hale wanted. But two nights ago, that era of suffering had ended. The part of the pack that defected after Draven's demise fought bravely alongside Ariel and Charlotte. The last battle was fierce, but in the end, it was Ariel that delivered the final blow to Draven's beta. Those that followed him went down easily after that.

As the celebration continued, the werewolves shifted back to their human forms, their laughter and cheers filling the night. They danced around a roaring bonfire, the flames casting flickering shadows on their faces. Ariel stood tall as he watched over his pack with pride. He knew that their victory was not just a physical one, but a triumph of their spirits. It was good to see so many familiar faces in the pack. He was home again.

Charlotte's eyes sparkled with excitement. She had been instrumental in the battle, using her agility and cunning to outmaneuver Hale's minions. Now she danced with abandon, her joy infectious. Ariel approached her, placing a hand on her shoulder.

"You fought pretty well," he said, his voice warm and filled with respect.

"You didn't do too bad yourself," she grinned.

"Tonight, we celebrate not just our freedom, but the strength and courage that lies within each of us."

"Yes, we did it together," she replied. "As a pack."

"Speaking of which, have you seen Caelum around?"

Again, she grinned, pointing at the door of one of the homes where Caelum was entering with a young female wolf. Before Ariel could go after him, Charlotte pulled him to her.

"Dance with me, Ariel. Let Caelum celebrate on his own this time."

Ariel grumbled. "But what if—"

"You worry too much. He'll be fine," she assured him. "Now dance with me."

"Fine," he sighed.

As the night wore on, the celebration continued.

A beautiful, female werewolf named Lila led Caelum into a modest home. He had caught her eye during the celebration, and she had caught his.

Through the eyes of a potential lover, she was a mesmerizing blend of wild beauty and fierce strength. Her eyes had a deep, amber glow with an inner fire that captivated and drew him in. A cascade of waves, her hair framed her face well and flowed down her back, catching the moonlight and shimmering like a midnight river. Her skin, though marked with the faint scars of past battles, was smooth and warm to the touch, a testament to her resilience and vitality.

She had asked him to dance with her, and he gladly obliged. Her movements were fluid and confident, each step a dance of primal elegance. She exuded an aura of mystery and allure, a wild spirit that could not be tamed, but was all the more enchanting for it.

Her presence was magnetic, drawing him closer with every glance and touch. There was a depth to her, a complexity that spoke of untold stories and hidden layers. She was a creature of the night, but in her eyes, he saw the promise of dawn, a new beginning filled with passion and adventure.

And he wanted her.

They were a mess of teeth and tongues as they entered the bedroom, tearing each other's clothes off. He tossed her onto the bed, a wicked smile on his face when she licked her lips. She happily welcomed him into her arms as he climbed on top of her.

"Are you sure you're all right with this?" he asked. "You know I'm not a wolf, right?"

"I know, and I don't care," she growled, kissing him before he asked another question.

Caelum understood the message and kissed her back. He blazed a trail of kisses down her neck to her breasts, taking one into his mouth and kneading the other with his hand. He lingered at her breast briefly before traveling. As he began to nip and suck and kiss his way down her body, he could smell the delectable scent of her desire from where he was—enticing him. Drawing him to his intended destination.

He settled himself between the V of her thighs, and inhaled deeply to take in her wild, feminine scent. It pleased him with how wet she already was. He gently pulled the slick, glistening folds of her arousal apart. Then he dipped his head, sweeping his tongue between them. He groaned. The wild taste of her flavor burst on his tongue. He could deny his need no longer.

Lila wriggled and moaned as he worked her into a state of hysteria, using long carnal licks. She helplessly laid beneath him, writhing and arching, as he teased her opening expertly. When she felt the lash of his tongue on her clit, she thought she would go mindless. Then his tongue swirled around the sensitive bud as a finger impaled the inside of her.

Caelum knew she would not last much longer with his oral assault. She needed her release. Grinning to himself, he shoved another finger inside of her, making her cry out and buck. He would make her scream for him. After all, he had earned it.

With one swift motion, he retracted his fingers. He took her rear in a firm grip and curled her hips, then he stabbed her core with his tongue. Her back arched as she gave a loud cry, but it was not the scream he wanted.

Her fingers laced through his hair, jerking uncomfortably, but he did not care. Not while she tasted so good, and she was making such delightful noises. So, he continued to fuck her with his tongue until she could no longer take it. With a deafening howl, she came undone on his tongue. A chorus of howls came from outside after hers.

She was panting hard when she looked down at him, a smug look on his face. "Where did you learn to do that?" she rasped.

He chuckled. "That's not all I can do," he said, his voice heavy with desire.

"Then show me your magic, demon," she purred.

"It will be as my lady wishes."

When he entered her, she sighed with contentment. His strokes were long and sensual. He wanted to please her more—to test his control. He could feel her life energy pour into him, but she did not seem to notice. Good. He would take what he needed and grant her a second profound release that would leave her spent.

The more he pumped into her—the harder his thrusts—the more she cried out. He was hitting every spot just right. When he lifted her legs to gain deeper access, she finally screamed the way he wanted. He felt her walls clamp down around him when she came again. She sucked him in so hard that it triggered his own release.

Caelum grunted as he let her have all that he had. Once he was done, he carefully pulled out of her. She had already fallen asleep by the time he laid down next to her. He fell asleep shortly after, his thoughts of training his new Dolls ever present in his mind.

Epilogue

Five years had passed since the fall of Kingston Hale. An investigation was done, and his allies were all outed and arrested. The authorities removed the public officials Hale had been blackmailing from office, and they were never heard from again. Things were quiet, better.

His one night with Lila turned into three, but after that, he refused to take her to his bed again. He let her down gently and told her why. She understood, but insisted on being one of his Dolls. He gladly granted her request, but under the condition that she would take other lovers before he began her training. He did not want her to go mad from being with him too often.

Caelum had established his Doll House a year after Hale's demise. Courtesans and prostitutes from all over London came to him to be trained as living Dolls. With Ariel's and Charlotte's help, Caelum had gained enough control that he did not need to feed as often or transform unwillingly when there was too much sexual energy around. He could train his Dolls with no need to feed.

There was also the occasional 'task' that Ximena had wanted done. He would have to get his hands dirty by getting rid of the vampire queen's adversaries. Something that did not sit well with him, but it was part of the blood pact he agreed to years ago.

Caelum purchased and renamed the Silver Stake to fit his own brand. He renamed it the Azure Veil, while his first House was called Delirium. The grand openings of both Houses were successful, which made Caelum elated. Roland visited a few times. His business was growing as well. There were those that did not perform well as Dolls for one reason or another, so Caelum offered them to Roland as blanks to use as he saw fit.

Soon, other brothels were converting into Doll Houses, some even sought Caelum's guidance, while others tried to be on their own and failed.

"I'm proud of you, Caelum," said Roland. "You've turned into a fine man."

Caelum nodded, raising his glass of wine. "Thank you."

"I still can't believe you summoned your father. Well done on banishing him."

Again, Caelum nodded as he sipped his drink.

Roland frowned at Caelum's lack of verbal responses. "Something on your mind?"

"There are several things on my mind, old man."

"Anything bothering you?" Roland pushed.

"Something my father said, but it's nothing," Caelum said, brushing off the subject.

"It's something if you're thinking about it," Roland countered.

Caelum sighed. He knew Roland would not let it go. "He said my new life wouldn't last, and that I can't escape my fate."

"I see."

"He also said you wouldn't save me a second time."

"Hmm," Roland murmured. "Fate is a fickle thing. I can't promise you a third chance at life. Death comes for all, but I can help you as much as I can."

At that, Caelum smiled wryly.

"I know that wasn't the answer you were seeking, but I am a god, and there is a balance to maintain."

"I understand," Caelum answered.

"Good," he said, standing. "I have to get going. I have my own business to take care of."

Caelum raised a curious brow. "Still dealing out death to those that deserve it?"

"Yes," he replied flatly.

"Fate is a fickle thing indeed," Caelum laughed.

Roland smiled and patted Caelum on the shoulder. "Just be happy and live well, Caelum. That's all you can do."

"Yes, sir."

"Be well, boy." He waved as he vanished into thin air like a specter.

Caelum continued to sit on the balcony of Delirium and drink alone. Roland was right. He just needed to be happy and live his life the best he could while keeping his secret.

A loud crash shook him from his thoughts. It sounded like glass breaking. He wondered if it was another drunk Ariel tossed out of a window for being too aggressive. Despite his success, there were still the occasional messes that needed to be cleaned. With an exasperated sigh, he set his drink down and went to investigate the commotion. He smiled as he did so, wondering what kind of life he was going to have from then on.

About the Author

Ember Drake is an American author from Columbia, South Carolina. She has been writing since the age of ten and has aspired to be a published author since. Ember has always had a love of dragons and wolves. As a joke, she was told that all she needed was to put them together and then she would be happy. This resulted in the creation of Raesh, who was modeled after her favorite former Power Ranger, Johnny Yong Bosch. Roland/Zaven was modeled after her favorite actor, Matt Ryan.

She had been working on the House of Ausher series since the age of seventeen. It was just three short stories that only included vampires and werewolves, both of which she is a huge fan of. The series evolved from terrible Backstreet Boys fan fiction about three brothers to what it is today.

Visit EmberDrakeAuthor.com for news and updates!

OTHER WORKS BY EMBER DRAKE